SOFA
SURFER

MALCOLM DUFFY is a Geordie, born and bred. His debut novel *Me Mam. Me Dad. Me.* was inspired by his time at Comic Relief visiting projects that support women and children who have suffered as a result of domestic abuse. It has so far won the YA category of the Sheffield Children's Book Award 2019, the Redbridge Children's Book Award 2019 and was shortlisted for the Waterstones Children's Prize 2019.

Also by Malcolm Duffy

Me Mam. Me Dad. Me.

SOFA
SURFER

Malcolm Duffy

To the Creedsons,
Enjoy a read on your sofa!

Malcolm D

ZEPHYR

First published in the UK in 2020 by Zephyr,
an imprint of Head of Zeus Ltd

Copyright © Malcolm Duffy, 2020

975312468

A catalogue record for this book is available from
the British Library.

ISBN (HB): 9781786697677
ISBN (E): 9781786697660

Typeset by Ed Pickford

Printed and bound in Great Britain by
CPI Group (UK) Ltd, Croydon CR0 4YY

Head of Zeus Ltd
5–8 Hardwick Street
London ECIR 4RG

WWW.HEADOFZEUS.COM

For Jann

'People drown, quietly, before our eyes,
all the time.'

— Ilsa J. Bick

One

You never forget the day you lose your home.

I lost mine on a Tuesday.

I'd been doing maths homework. Evaluating exponents. Torture.

'Tyler,' shouted Mum.

'What?' I grunted, more to me than her.

'Tyler,' she cried again.

Guess it must be dinner. Or I've left a shoe lying around somewhere. Not bothered, really. Anything that stops maths is good to me. I closed my books, went downstairs, and looked in the dining room. Nobody there. No knives or forks or placemats out. Must be something else.

'We're in here.'

I dragged myself into the sitting room. As soon as I set foot inside I knew something wasn't right. For a start, Mum and Dad were sitting, squidged tight together on the sofa, holding hands and smiling: something they only do when they've been drinking. What made it stranger was that they didn't seem relaxed. They were perched right on the edge, as if there was something exciting on TV, which there wasn't. It was Sky News, with the sound off.

'Sit down,' said Dad.

I flopped on to a chair. Tallulah, my little sister, was already sitting cross-legged on the floor. The air was crackling with anticipation. For the first time ever I realised that the gold clock on the mantelpiece made a ticking sound.

'What's happened?'

'It's not what's happened. It's what will happen,' said Mum, squeezing Dad's hand, as they looked at each other with faces still debating whether to be happy or sad.

'We're going to move,' said Dad. From his voice, from his expression, from his body language, from everything, I got the impression I wasn't going to like what came next.

'Up north,' said Mum.

The oxygen level in the room dropped as Tallulah and I took in two extra-large portions of breath.

'Up north?' said Tallulah.

Mum and Dad nodded in unison.

The clock on the mantelpiece could not have ticked any louder.

'Why?' I asked.

'I've been offered a job in Bradford.'

'Where's that?' said Tallulah.

'Yorkshire.'

'Where's that?' said Tallulah.

They clearly weren't big on geography in Year Four.

'It's a big county. Up past Gran and Grandad's house.'

I stared at the TV. The presenter looked as if they were in a fish tank, mouthing silent words. I half-expected a banner to appear along the bottom: *Breaking news: the Jackson family to leave London.* I'd once got hit smack in the face by a ball in the playground. My parents' announcement was comparable to this.

Tick. Tock.

Over the last few months I'd heard them talking about properties and job opportunities and stuff like that. But that's all I thought it was – talk. Didn't for one second think the talk would actually turn into anything meaningful, like action. Mum and Dad aren't exactly the intrepid type. Dad's an accountant. His big love is golf, which is also his big hate, judging by the look on his face when he comes back. Mum works in HR, which I think is where you deal with people who hate their jobs. So why did they have to go and be vaguely adventurous?

'Well, say something,' said Mum.

But it's hard to find words when your brain's out of order.

I finally found one, hiding in a corner.

'When?'

Mum took a big breath. 'Your dad starts work in three months. I'm going to find a new job. In the meantime we'll start searching for a new home.'

Tick. Tock.

'But we've got a home.'

Mum and Dad swapped looks, as if to say, *Who's going to take this one?* Mum stepped up to the plate.

'Tyler, your dad's been given a great opportunity. We're both really stressed out working in London. It'll be a new start for all of us. Also, the air quality here's not getting any better. It'll do my asthma the world of good to get out of town. And we'll be nearer Gran and Grandad in Derby.'

She'd obviously been working on that list.

'And then there's the crime,' she continued.

'What crime?'

'It's all around us. A boy got stabbed in Richmond last week.'

'Three stops away on the tube. Big deal.'

'It was a pretty big deal for his parents.'

Mum gets worked up about stuff like that. Even cries at the news sometimes.

'Where will we live?' said Tallulah.

'We'll find somewhere nice,' said Mum, smiling at Dad for support. 'Maybe a village somewhere.'

'A village?' I spat, with as much disgust as I could muster.

'Or a small town.'

'I don't want to go.'

'Lots of families move.'

'Lots of families stay put. I want to stay here.'

Dad looked at Mum, as if to say, *Told you he'd be a nightmare.*

'You've got to give it a chance.'

But I didn't want to give Yorkshire a chance. I didn't want to give anywhere a chance. I wanted to stay here. Where I live. I'd heard enough. Got to my feet and stomped towards the door.

'Tyler,' exclaimed Mum. 'We haven't finished.'

But I had.

Went upstairs as noisily as I could, kicked open the door to my room, swept all my maths books off my desk and fell backwards on to my bed. How could they do this to me? I've got everything I want here. Everything. My squad: Ben, Asher, Tom, Lucas, Reggie, Mason. Brentford FC, a bus ride away. A school I don't hate anywhere near enough to want to leave. And last but not least, I've got London, the city with a squillion things to do. The place everyone wants to move to. So what do we do? Leave it for some crumbling village, up north.

I put my hand against the wall. I don't think it's possible to love a wall, but I loved this one, and the three I couldn't quite reach, and the bedroom door, and the floor and the windows and the ceiling. It wasn't the greatest house in the world, but I suddenly realised how much it meant to me. It was part of my life. A picture popped up in my mind. Me in the hall, in a Moses basket, one day old. It's the only home I've ever known.

I took my hand off the wall and put it to my face. The cool felt good. My face was burning. Didn't think I could get emotional over a house, but that's what their news had done to me. Tears began to escape. They didn't want to go to Yorkshire either. They wanted to stay here, where they belonged. But I knew deep down it wasn't going to happen. I'd seen the looks on Mum and Dad's faces. They'd made their minds up. We were leaving.

Two

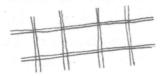

Fast-forward six months.

I now live in Ilkley, West Yorkshire.

And I hate it.

Our new house has all the usual stuff – front door, windows, drainpipes, roof, rooms. It's also got something else, a stupid name – *Fairview*. Maybe it had a fair view once, when it was built by the Victorians or whoever. Now it's got a view of a road and three lock-up garages. But Mum and Dad love it. Or they seem to love it. Don't really care. All I know is that my home is over three hundred kilometres from where it should be.

Our house isn't the only thing screwing up my life. It also happens to be the start of the summer holidays. What's wrong with that? This is what's wrong with that: I'm faced with weeks and weeks of nothingness, trapped in a place where excitement has been abolished, with no mates whatsoever. Well, not entirely true. I have made two friends, Dom Kingham and Jack Goddard, but right now they may as well be enemies. Dom's gone to his parents' house in France for the entire summer, and while Jack's still here, he might as well not be. The only thing I can rely on him for is being unreliable. We arrange to meet. He cancels. We fix up a game online. He's busy. I think while he's number one on my new friend list, I'm at the bottom of his. I only get a look-in when his other mates are busy. Probably in his contacts as *TLR: Tyler, Last Resort*.

I miss my old home like mad.

Might sound a bit odd, but I took photos of all the rooms before we left, and every now and then, I lie on my bed and look at them on my phone, remembering everything that went on there. The kitchen window I broke with a football. The sitting room, where I found my badly wrapped bike one Christmas morning. My bedroom, where I used to hang out for hours with my mates, my real mates. The downstairs cupboard, where I used to throw my school jacket. The bathroom with the toilet I puked in when I got gastroenteritis.

I didn't tell Mum and Dad about the photos. They'd only go mad.

Tyler, you've got to move on.

Where to?

Thought I might have got over it by now. But I haven't. Even though the rooms are familiar, I still hate them, like kids in class you can't get on with, no matter how hard you try. It's as though our old house has died and I'm the only one who's sad.

Mum's got a new job. Always said she wanted to work from home, and now she does, as a content moderator for some social media company. Has to watch all that horrible stuff online she won't let me watch, then tell someone to take it down. From the look on her face by tea time, she's more stressed than she ever was in London. Not that she'd ever admit it.

Dad's also got a new job and works really long hours. The country doesn't seem to have done much to relax him, and he turns into Mr Moody when he gets home. At weekends, he goes walking after a golf ball with some neighbours.

The family member who's most in love with Ilkley is Tallulah. She seems to have made friends with just about every single seven-year-old in town, and her summer comprises a diary full of play dates. Good for you, little sis.

But Mum was right about one thing. In half a year of living in West Yorkshire none of us has been stabbed.

There was something else good to come out of moving up here.

Dexter.

When we moved, Mum and Dad promised we could get a dog. As bribes go, it was champion, as Yorkshire people say. I've even put him in the contact list on my phone, with a made-up number. Loneliness does weird things to you.

Time for one of his walks.

In the kitchen, there he is, ever-ready Dexter, tail wagging, eyes wide open, tongue unfolded, waiting to go. It's all you have to do to make a dog happy. Open a door. Dexter's a Border Collie. Farmers often use them as sheep dogs. Not that we have any sheep. The only thing he has to herd is me.

I grabbed his lead from a hook on the wall and walk outside.

'Bye, Fairspew.'

We went down the street, and across the fields towards the River Wharfe, me at a trot, Dexter as if he'd been shot from a canon. We reached a big wooden gate, but before I could open it, Dexter was already on the other side, squeezing flat on his belly and squirming through, desperate to reach the open space. We crossed Riverside Gardens, Dexter darting this way and that, but never far from my feet, as if attached by an invisible string.

'You love it here, don't you?'

Dexter's tongue flopped out. Dog speak for, *Yes, you idiot.*

Fields and woods and hills and lakes and streams. Perfect if you have four legs. Not so perfect if you have two. And you're fifteen. And friendless. And bored.

'Want to chase sticks?'

That's the most stupid thing you've ever said, Tyler.

I found a big stick and threw it as far as I could. Within seconds it was back at my feet, covered in slobber, ready to be launched again.

'Wonder what my friends in Chiswick are doing now?'

Dexter looked at me. Clueless.

I used to FaceTime them, but not any more. Just too painful. Seeing them, but not being able to be with them. Hearing about the things they'd done, reminding me of all the things I hadn't done. Mum says we can go and visit them some time, but that would be torture too. A few hours, when what I'm really after is weeks. And then heading back up the M1. In slow-moving traffic.

'I still hate them for what they've done. What do you think of my parents, Dex?'

Dexter squatted and did a poo.

I laughed.

Briefly.

I'd forgotten the poo bags.

I looked around to see if anyone had spotted Dexter's curly calling card. Luckily there was no one near, and I hurried away. Probably get arrested here for doing something like that.

We crossed the bridge over the River Wharfe and past the rugby club.

'Can you believe we're not even going on holiday this year?'

Dexter seemed happy at this news. No kennels for him.

'How could they choose a new kitchen over two weeks in Spain?'

Unable to answer, Dexter ran off.

Typical. The one year I most wanted to get away, we stay put. Mum had her heart set on an island with a granite top, twin sinks, and cupboards. I had my heart set on a different sort of island. Mum won.

What was I going to do? While I loved Dexter, I couldn't walk him every minute of every day. His paws would be down to stumps by September. I needed to find something else to fill my days. Something that didn't cost much. Something that maybe gave me the chance to meet someone. The answer came a few minutes later.

As we turned into Denton Road, I saw a white building in the distance, surrounded by a wall. A place where many hours could be happily killed.

Ilkley Lido and Pool.

Three

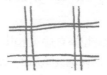

As a watery sun did its best to try and warm West Yorkshire, I crawled my way up and down the lido, reaching out as far as I could, fingers slightly splayed, before drawing back, down towards my stomach, hand skimming my hip, breaking free, elbow soft, arm loose, ready to ease into the water, like an arm going into a sleeve, to start the whole process over again.

Swimming's what I'm best at. Trust me to have a hobby you do on your own, staring down at slow-moving tiles. Can't even talk to anyone, unless you want a bellyful of water. But I enjoy it, and with weeks of nothing ahead of me, at least the lido's somewhere to go.

Fifty lengths later I was done and, breathing hard, climbed from the pool and hurried over to my towel. My circulation had ground to a halt, but after some serious rubbing I persuaded it to move again. I sat down and looked around to see if there was anyone I knew.

There weren't many people about, though. A constant stream of clouds and a cool breeze had seen to that. In fact, there was only one person even close to my age. A few metres away on the grass was a teenage girl. She looked cool. Her jeans were less like jeans, just big holes held together by denim. She wore a baggy T-shirt and white trainers. And while one arm was white, the other was multicoloured, decorated in big swirly tattoos.

With nothing else to do I snatched another look at her. She wore glasses. Her hair was dark, shoulder-length. She was tall, slim, with a nice enough face, and looked about eighteen, though it's hard to tell sometimes. But I know for certain that eighteen-year-olds aren't the least bit interested in boys my age.

'Dead canny swimmer, yous.'

I turned, startled to see she was talking to me.

'Me?'

'Aye, yous.'

'Thanks,' I muttered.

She must have been watching. Clearly even more bored than me.

'Where's ya yhem?'

'Sorry?'

'Ya home,' she said, replacing the 'o' of home with dozens of unnecessary 'u's.

'Here.'

'You live in a lido?'

'No, I live in Ilkley. Where you from?'

'Can yous not tell?'

Sort of.

'Tyneside,' she said.

Even further from London.

'What's ya name?'

'Tyler.'

'As in bathroom tiler?'

My lips didn't move a millimetre. That joke was like chalk, worn away to nothing, after years of use.

This wasn't what I wanted. I'd hoped to meet someone from round here, someone from school maybe, someone my age. I had another quick squint to see if there was anyone fitting that description, but, no, they were all abroad, hurling themselves into warm water. Apart from a few mums and young kids, it was just us.

'You're not from roond here?'

Didn't want to talk to her. But had nothing better to do.

'No, London. Family dragged me up here.'

'Never been to London, me.'

I wondered who she was. The Geordie didn't seem like one of your typical Ilkley tourists: middle-aged men and women in shorts and boots about to take on the moor, well-dressed families about to stuff themselves on scones at one of the tea rooms, or coach parties coming to the Winter Garden to catch an act no longer good enough for TV.

She'd probably come for the day, and having got here, wished she hadn't. Probably bored stiff, just like me.

'Do you live here?' I asked.

She chewed a nail, as if struggling with the question, even though it was the easiest one I could think of.

'Hope to.'

No idea what she meant by that.

She looked away, towards the entrance, a worried expression on her face. But the worry was clearly passing through, because she turned to me again and smiled. 'I knaa it's a bit cheeky, Tyler, but I've gorra question for yous.'

'What?' I said, fiddling with the blue locker key on my wrist.

Never in a thousand years could I have imagined what she said next.

'Will you teach me to swim?'

Four

'Didn't they teach you swimming at school?'

'Only exercise we got was from fighting.'

From the look on her face this wasn't a joke.

'Why not get lessons from the swim coaches?' I said, looking at a young lifeguard, sitting in a tall chair on the poolside. 'They'll have forms at reception. Just fill in your details.'

'I divvent dee details. And they'll charge a fortune. D'ya think I'm made of money?'

To be honest she didn't look like the daughter of a Russian billionaire.

'Doesn't have to be lengths. Widths'll do.'

Wasn't sure. I'm a good swimmer, but I'd never taught anyone anything in my life.

'I'll pay yous.'

Three words that changed everything.

One thing I needed, apart from a holiday and friends, was money. I had my ears set on a new pair of headphones. I'd seen an ad for the brand I wanted on YouTube. They looked sick. Swimming is something I can do with my eyes closed. And she looked keen, make that borderline desperate, to learn.

'How much?'

Her eyes screwed up so tight you'd think she'd taken her glasses off.

'What aboot a fiver?'

I snorted. No idea how much swimming lessons cost, but they've got to be more than that.

'Ten.'

She put her maths face on.

'Seven-fifty.'

I should have gone to reception to check how much they charge, but didn't want her to go and find someone else.

'Okay, seven-fifty for every half-hour.'

'Half-hour?' she blurted. 'Thought it would be an hour.'

'Have you ever been in Ilkley Lido?' I said, adding extra weight to the word 'in'. She shook her head. 'Believe me, half an hour is more than enough.'

She grinned and held out a slim hand. I shook it quickly.

'See yous at the pool the morrow,' she said, once again adding an extra letter to 'you' and amputating the letters 'to' from tomorrow. Shame she didn't come with autocorrect.

'Ten o'clock?'

'Aye.'

She got to her feet and walked away.

'By the way, what's your name?'

'Me name's Spider.'

I was going to teach a Spider to swim. How mad is that?

In the town where nothing ever happens something had just happened. A girl with a tattooed arm and a strange voice wanted me to teach her to swim. I'd been swimming that long I couldn't ever remember a day I couldn't do it. It was so easy. But teaching it was a different matter.

When I got home I googled 'how to teach someone to swim'. It looked fairly straightforward. All about confidence, and the Geordie girl didn't seem lacking in that department. And she looked fairly fit. My biggest fear was that she'd be a complete natural, dive in and start powering up the pool doing tumble-turns after each length. Seven pounds fifty. Wouldn't get a very good pair of headphones for that. I'd make sure I taught her really slowly.

I don't normally tell my mum what I'm up to, but on this occasion I did. Thought she'd be well impressed. After all, she'd been nagging me for ages to get a summer job, and that's exactly what I'd done. But I must have picked the wrong moment. She'd had a bad morning watching people post nasty stuff online. Mum looked like she'd seen a ghost.

'You're not trained,' she said, as she watched me throw my towel in the washing machine.

'Mum, I know how to swim.'

'Just 'cos you can do it doesn't mean you can teach it.'

I threw in a sigh and a big shoulder slump.

'And who is this girl anyway?'

Good question.

'Someone who hangs out at the lido.'

'How old is she?'

'About eighteen, I think.'

'They must do swimming lessons there.'

'She doesn't want them.'

'Surely she'd want a professional, someone with all the badges and stuff.'

'Maybe she hates teachers.'

Mum thought as she looked out of the kitchen window at our small, neat garden.

'They have lifeguards, don't they?'

'Heaps.'

But I could tell from her face she wasn't convinced.

'She's not going to drown, Mum. The pool's not even a metre deep.'

'There's a deeper bit.'

'Which we'll be avoiding.'

She stared right through me as though I was glass. Couldn't tell whether she was thinking about me, or what she'd seen on her laptop.

'You wanted me to get a summer job.'

She snapped out of her trance.

'Yes, I did.'

She walked slowly over to me and took my hands, staring deep into my eyes. The stare made me look away.

'Okay, you can do it. But please be careful, Tyler.'

Five

Next morning I was outside the lido, mouth dryer than a day-old sandwich, trying to remember what I'd read online. After a few minutes kicking stones I spotted Spider approaching across the car park. She'd swapped her baggy T-shirt for an even baggier sweatshirt and her ever-so-holey jeans for some brightly coloured shorts, revealing two of the skinniest white legs I'd ever clapped eyes on. Maybe that's why she's called Spider.

'Hi, Tyler.'

'Hi, Spi … der.' Felt stupid saying it. Sounded like a lead guitarist in a thrash metal band. 'Why are you called Sp … ider?'

'It's Spider, all one word.'

'Yes, why are you called that?'

'Just am.'

Spider seemed a bit jittery. Probably nervous about the lesson.

'Howaay, then, let's gan swimmin'.'

I flashed my season ticket at the front desk and was surprised to see Spider do the same. I'd never seen her at the lido until the other day. It meant she wasn't here on holiday.

'So you live in Ilkley, then?'

She ignored my question and quickly put the pass away in her pocket. 'See yous by the pool,' she said, and hurried off to the ladies' changing room.

I changed quickly, put my towel in a bag, and went outside, scanning the lido. Once again, couldn't spot anyone even vaguely familiar. My guess was the kids from Ilkley Grammar would turn up late summer when they had tans to compare. For once I was glad I didn't know anybody. They'd all want to know why I was giving swimming lessons to a paper-white Geordie, and they'd stand by the side of the pool taking the pee.

A few moments later, Spider herself appeared. She was wearing an all-in-one swimsuit that could have fitted two of her. It was several sizes too big. The swimsuit revealed her body inking only went as far as one arm. Maybe it got too painful. Or she'd run out of money.

Her face looked different. Funny how just taking glasses off can do that. She looked at me through two tiny arrow slits.

'Tyler.'

'Yes, that's me,' I said. 'Are you ready?'

'Aye, just a bit nervous.'

Not the only one. It seemed weird to be teaching someone, especially when they're older than you, and you don't know them, and they're a girl.

'Got your goggles?'

Spider shook her head. I took mine out of the swim bag and gave them to her. She slipped them on.

'Have yous not got any with prescription lenses?'

'No,' I snapped.

Don't think I'll ever make a teacher.

'Let's start in this bit,' I said, nodding my head in the direction of the fountain, where two little kids were busy kicking water at each other, letting out ear-splitting screams.

Spider walked slowly around to the shallow end and dipped a toe in. The dipping didn't last long.

'Fog me, it's freezin'. Isn't there anywhere with warm water roond here?'

I looked over at a building with scaffolding around it. 'There was, until a few weeks ago. They're doing repairs. The indoor pool won't open until November.'

Disappointment leaked on to Spider's face, and she shivered as she looked down at the uninviting liquid. 'Take a canny few kettles to warm this up.'

'Still want to do an hour?'

'Divvent think I'll last a minute in this,' said Spider, her voice vibrating with the cold.

She gritted her teeth and eased her thin legs into

the water, letting out little bursts of air as she went. I followed her into the pool, trying not to show her how cold I thought it was.

'Not so bad,' I lied.

Spider stood, arms wrapped tight around her chest, body shaking, teeth chattering. I needed to get a move on. Google didn't mention what to do if the person you were teaching had a heart attack.

'First off, you need to get used to putting your face in the water.'

'Why?'

'You just do.'

Spider slowly got down on all fours in the shallow water, then buried her face beneath the surface. A second or so later she reappeared, coughing and spluttering.

'It's gan doon the wrong way,' she said, gasping.

'Did you hold your breath?'

Spider shook her head.

This was going to be a long half-hour.

'You're not a fish, Spider. When you go underwater, breathe out. When you run out of air, come up for some more.'

After composing herself Spider gave it another go. She was more successful second time round.

'That's berra. But I can't see for bubbles.'

'That's because you're not moving. When you swim you leave the bubbles behind.'

'Dead complicated, this.'

'Let's go where it's a bit deeper.'

The instructions suggested holding someone's hand to give them confidence. Apart from Tallulah and my mum, I'd never held a girl's hand before. Shaken a few, but never held one. First time for everything. I held my hands out, and Spider gladly took them, gripping so tight you'd think she was water-skiing.

'Okay?'

'It's that bloody freezing I'll be walking on it soon.'

I led her deeper into the pool.

'The main thing is to enjoy it. Think of it as your friend,' I said, letting go of her and moving my hands through the water.

'Friends like this I can dee without,' she gasped, moving one white and one multicoloured arm quickly through the water.

'Okay, that's enough splashing. Now hold the side of the pool and kick your legs.'

I've watched people inch their way into the lido. Spider millimetred her way in. But after enough swear words to get you excluded, she was finally up to her chest, the water making her swimsuit saggier than ever.

'I-I-I'm in,' she gasped. 'Can I get out now?'

'No. Now hold on to the side and kick your legs.'

Spider grabbed the wall and started kicking like fury. For the first time I got a good look at the tattoos on her arm. They consisted of several flowery swirls surrounding two words – *Me mam.*

I'd brought a kick board with me and handed it to Spider.

'I'll never fit on that,' she said, looking at the small polystyrene float.

'Just hold it out at arm's length and kick.'

Spider held on to the board and began to cross the pool.

'I'm moving.'

'That's 'cos you're walking.'

After several failed attempts she finally managed to raise her legs from the bottom and began to kick. Great plumes of spray went everywhere as she edged her way across the pool.

'Think I'm getting seasick,' she gasped. 'Can we stop now?'

'Okay. Lesson over.'

Spider left the pool a thousand times faster than she'd got in. She ran over the grassy area to her bag and began defrosting herself with a towel. I hurried after her and started towelling my legs as hard as I could. I looked over at Spider. She'd taken my goggles off and had a pained expression on her face. Or it could just have been the squinting from lack of glasses.

'You did okay.'

'Ta.'

I considered going back to the changing room but decided against it. After all, I had nothing else to do. It seemed Spider didn't have a packed diary either, as she sat there trying to make the most of what little sunshine was coming our way. But it didn't look like the rays had cheered her up. That worried expression was there again.

'Do you like living here?'

Spider put her glasses back on and looked at the woods behind the lido. 'Aye. Better than some places I've been.'

'You travel a lot, do you?'

She nodded, but from her face the travelling hadn't exactly been enjoyable.

'Where've you been?'

'Places.'

Spider would make a great spy.

'I hate living here.'

She turned to me, suddenly angry. 'You've gorra house, haven't you, a bedroom, heating, food for dinner? Then you've got bugger all to be hacked off aboot.'

Don't know what had rattled her. I'd only said I hated living here. Decided to talk about something else.

'Why do you want to learn to swim?'

Spider looked over at the moor, now capped with a large black cloud. She went quiet for a bit before speaking.

'Doctor said it would be good for me.'

'A doctor?'

'Aye, said it would calm me doon.'

'What do you need to calm doon, sorry, down for?'

There followed an even longer silence.

'You won't tell anyone?'

That was a joke. Who was I going to tell, apart from a one-year-old sheep dog?

'Cross my heart.'

'I get panic attacks.'

Six

• •

Unless you're scared of tea rooms, I couldn't see anything in Ilkley to panic about.

'Why do you get attacks?'

'Think me body hates me.'

'Are they scary?'

She nodded.

Maybe that was why Spider acted nervous, not knowing when the panic might creep up and attack her. Be bad if it happened during one of our sessions. Might be the end of her lessons. And my headphones.

'Do you work in Ilkley?'

But the question remained just that. She stood up. 'See yous the same time the morrow, Tyler.'

'What about the money? You did bring the money?' I asked anxiously, as though I was about to have a panic attack of my own.

Spider shrugged her bony shoulders.

'You promised.'

'I know I did, Tyler, man. And I will. Do I look like someone who doesn't pay their way?'

You do, actually.

'I'll pay yous.'

Realised I didn't know who on earth Spider was or where she lived or what she did. Maybe she was lying about her panic attacks. Maybe she was lying about the money. Maybe she was lying about everything.

I should have googled 'how to win an argument'.

'I need the money,' I said, as loudly as I dared, without attracting attention.

'Keep your hair on, man.'

'Please, just bring the money.'

'I'll bring it next time.'

'And bring next time's money as well.'

''Course.'

Spider grabbed her bag and wet towel. I watched as her skinny legs took her back to the changing rooms. Perhaps she'd asked a load of other kids at the lido about lessons and I was the only one stupid enough to say yes. I went home praying I hadn't been duped.

Mum must have had enough of the internet. She was on her knees, planting some flowers in the front garden. She looked up as the gate squeaked open.

'How did it go?'

Shrug.

'Words, Tyler.'

'Okay.'

'Don't sound very excited.'

That's because excitement requires something exciting to happen.

'Did you teach her anything?'

'Taught her that you need to keep moving in Ilkley Lido or you'll die.'

Mum smiled. Briefly.

'You don't seem very happy.'

'She forgot the money.'

Mum sat up on her haunches and took off her gardening gloves. She had her concerned look on, the one she saves for me. 'That's not good, Tyler. What does she do?'

Shrug.

'Well, does she go to college? Is she working?'

Double shrug.

'Is she from round here?'

'No, Tyneside.'

'Maybe here for her holidays.'

'She's got a season pass.'

'Maybe not, then.' Mum scraped a bit of dirt from her glove. 'But she's a nice person?'

'Think so.'

Didn't want to tell her about Spider having a go at me for moaning.

'Well, if that's the case, she'll pay you.'

Spider did pay me the next day. Five pounds. I'll never win any maths prizes but even I know that seven point five times two does not equal five.

'I'll bring the rest the morrow.'

'I want it now,' I shouted, not caring who heard.

'I haven't gorrit, man.'

A groan of frustration escaped from my chest. I thought girls her age all had debit cards, or tins under their bed with 'Rainy Day Fund' on it, or parents to borrow cash from. How could she not have the money?

I was tempted to cancel the lesson, but three things stopped me. First, I had five pounds more than I had yesterday. Second, I felt sorry for Spider and her panic attacks. Third, I finally had someone to hang out with. Okay, three and a half. She came out with funny stuff. I'd never heard girls come out with the sort of things Spider says. Some in our class have taken up swearing as an after-school hobby, and others show funny stuff on their phones, which is not the same as being funny. But Spider says things that are unique.

'Here comes Batman. What's that make me – Bobbin?'

I'd brought my wetsuit with me. I zipped it up and joined Spider, who was busy shivering in the shallow end.

'How come I divvent get one?'

''Cos I'm standing still. Okay, go back to kicking from the wall. That'll warm you up.'

As Spider splashed away, I remembered what the next lesson was about, getting someone to kick while lying on their back. To achieve that meant I'd have to put my hand underneath her. More physical contact.

'Excuse me, Spider, do you mind if I put my hand on your back?'

She laughed. 'God, you're so posh. The lads at me old school were like octopuses. Mind you, divvent think they ever tried to touch me back.'

'It's so I can support you,' I said, feeling the heat radiating from my cheeks.

''Course you can, man. Anything's better than drowning.'

I got Spider to turn around and hold the wall with her hands, while I placed my hand under her back. She was surprisingly light, like carrying a very long, damp tray.

'Dead clever, yous.'

Cutting and pasting an article into your head doesn't make you clever, but I didn't turn the compliment down. Don't get that many.

Having moved her up and down the pool a few times, I took her into a slightly deeper part to try treading water, which Spider totally failed to master. No sooner had her feet left the bottom than they were back down again, like a couple of anchors.

'Thought the water would dilute gravity, but it

makes it worse,' said Spider, as she tried and failed to lift her feet.

'It'll come with practice.'

'Can I gerroot now?' she said, wrapping her long arms around her, and twitching with the cold.

I looked at my watch. We'd only done twenty minutes. But she was paying for it.

'Sure.'

Spider waded through the water, dashed over to her towel and began rubbing her legs furiously.

'Eeh, that's better,' she said, sitting down and angling her face towards the sun, the way I've noticed girls do. 'It's dead good of yous to give your time up for me. You must have shed loads of friends roond here.'

My laugh said it all.

'Not shed loads?'

I played with a blade of grass. 'Had plenty back in London.'

'Miss the place, divvent ya?'

Nod.

'Gorra move on, man. You cannit cling to what's gone. The past is like breakfast. It's never coming back. Unless you throw up.'

I laughed. Even Spider smiled at her little joke.

'Bet your mam and dad had good reasons to come up here.'

'Good reasons for them.'

I didn't want to talk about my mum and dad. Not after what they'd done.

'Did *your* parents bring you here?'

Spider looked at a young couple trying to play ping pong. The ball seemed to be going everywhere but the table.

'Me mam's dead.'

Guess that's why she'd got the shrine on her arm. I'd never met anyone whose parents had died before. Didn't know what to say.

'I'm sorry.'

Spider nodded.

'Did it hurt?'

'When me mam died?'

'No, the tattoo.'

Spider glanced at her arm. 'Not really.' She looked away, like people do when they don't want you to see they're sad.

'What did she die of?'

'Cancer.'

They're always collecting for cancer. But it keeps on getting people.

'What about your dad?'

'He's not dead.' Spider played with a corner of her towel. 'But I wish he was.'

'Why?'

Spider kept her words locked away. Something bad

must have happened. Just like the bad thing that had happened to me.

'What do you do, then?'

Spider looked sad. Not sure why. Only asked what she did. Maybe she wanted a job and couldn't get one, or maybe she'd got the sack, or maybe she had an embarrassing job, like a toilet cleaner, and didn't want me to know.

She changed the subject.

'S'pose you'll be off on your holidays soon?'

'No,' I spat. 'My family have gone for kitchen cupboards and sliding drawers this year. Oh, the fun we'll have opening and closing them.'

'I'd love a kitchen, me.'

'Do you like cooking?'

'Prefer eating.'

We both smiled.

'Are you going away anywhere?'

She shook her head.

'Though I'd like to gan reet up there one day,' she said, staring across the valley to the moor. 'On those rocks with the little figures on top.'

Even from the town you could see the tiniest people in the world silhouetted against the sky.

'Yeah, the Cow and Calf Rocks. They should be called the Cow and Carve Rocks. There's that many names carved into them.'

'Must be a belter of a view up there.'

'Not bad.'

'There's a song aboot it, ye knaa. "On Ilkla Moor Baht'At". It's the Yorkshire National Anthem.'

'Thought only countries had anthems.'

'Yorkshire people think this is a country. Or should be. Me cousin's boyfriend's from here. Says Yorkshire should be independent. So what brilliant song do they choose? One about being on a moor without a hat.'

She looked at me, her face a closed book. But then she said something, a thing I wasn't expecting.

'I'm dead grateful for what you're deein, Tyler. Dead grateful. You've no idea what this means to me.'

And with that she picked up her stuff and hurried off.

Seven

When I got home I texted Jack to see if he wanted to play *Seek and Annihilate*. To my amazement he said yes. But the amazement and the annihilation didn't last long. We'd only been playing for an hour when he messaged to say he had to go to his gran's. Jack always does this when he's not winning.

I nearly messaged back, *LOSER!* followed by ten thumbs-down emojis, but didn't want to sacrifice fifty per cent of my friends over a stupid war game. So I wrote: *Let's play tomorrow.*

To which he replied: *Maybe.*

Typical Jack. Another example of TLR at work.

And so, with no one to annihilate, I took Dexter for a long walk, then came back for dinner.

Dad was home, in one of his thirty-over-par golf moods.

'Set the table, Tyler,' he barked.

One reason Dad said he wanted to leave London was

to spend more time with us. Guess what? We see less of him than ever. And the Dad we finally see isn't the one we want. Tired, grumpy, moaning about his boss, people he works with, his workload, traffic. All he's now got time for is whacking a golf ball and shouting at us.

'I want to watch TV.'

'We are having family dinner,' he said, like a ventriloquist, through gritted teeth.

Mum had read somewhere that families who eat dinner together are much happier.

Failed to see how sitting at a table with the two people who'd ruined my life was going to make me happy, but there you go.

'Great,' I huffed, clanking the knives and forks on to the table, to show how much I enjoyed this little task.

Mum grabbed some plates from a cupboard. The cupboard refused to shut, so she slammed it hard and the door fell off.

I laughed.

Mum didn't, huffing as she picked the door up from the floor.

'I will be so glad when we've got our new kitchen.'

They'll probably throw a party. I'll make sure I've got homework that night. The kitchen that ruined my summer.

Dad placed a molten bowl of chilli con carne on the

table and Mum appeared with a bowl of rice and a plate of garlic bread. She poured two large glasses of red wine for her and Dad. Mum took a huge gulp of wine and looked at an empty chair.

'Tallulah, dinner's ready. Wash your hands.'

'I'm going to use a knife and fork,' came the reply.

'Just do it,' shouted Dad.

Whoever did the research into family dinners had never eaten with the Jacksons.

We all waited for Tallulah to wash her sticky digits and a moment later she came bouncing into the dining room.

'Why are we eating at the table?' she asked, staring at it as though an alien craft had landed.

'So we can have a nice conversation about kitchens,' I said.

Mum and Dad rolled their eyes. Sometimes think they wish they'd left me behind in London. I wish they had.

The mince, beans and rice were doled out and we sat looking at each other in silence, the way happy families do.

'Your mum and I have been talking.'

I put my fork down and slowed my chewing. This was usually the prelude to bad news. *Your mum and I have been talking. We're moving up north. Your mum and I have been talking. We're not going on holiday this year.* If only they'd stop talking to each other, my life would be ten times better.

'Are we going to Disneyland?' said Tallulah hopefully.

'No, we're not going to Disneyland,' said Mum, wiping sauce from her lips. 'We've been talking about Tyler.'

'Must have been boring,' said my charming little sister.

'Tallulah,' Mum scolded.

I put my knife and fork down and waited to discover what the talk had been about. I had the feeling this was going straight into my top ten worst family dinners of all time. Dad did a pretend cough, the type teachers do when they want your attention. 'Mum says you've been giving someone swimming lessons.'

Tallulah laughed. Mum put a finger to her lips and my sister managed to stifle her snigger.

'What's wrong with that?'

'You're not qualified. We want you to stop.'

I folded my arms and blew garlic breath in their direction.

'But you're the ones who keep saying I need a summer job.'

'Yes,' said Dad. 'A proper job.'

'You can't get proper jobs at fifteen.'

'There are lots of things you can do,' said Mum. 'Dog walking, paper delivering, car washing.'

'Sod that.'

'Tyler, do not speak to your mother like that,' boomed Dad, slamming his palm down hard on the tablecloth.

'I didn't call her a sod, I said sod that.'

Dad continued to glare at me as though there was only one sod in the room. Me.

'I'm teaching a girl to swim. Would you rather I let her drown?'

'She can borrow my old armbands.'

'Hush, Tallulah,' said Mum.

'If something goes wrong, you'll be in big trouble,' exclaimed Dad. 'Have you done first aid? Do you know the recovery position? And what if she panics and pulls you under?'

'I'm not teaching her in the North Sea. This is Ilkley Lido.'

'I've spoken to Mrs Driver,' said Mum. 'They're going to Turkey. They need someone to water their plants and feed their cats.'

'I don't like plants and I don't like cats.'

'I don't like having to drive into Bradford every day and work silly hours, but I do it. To earn money.'

Yes, Dad, but not enough money to have a holiday and *a kitchen.* I kept these words behind my teeth. My parents both had knives in their hands.

'No,' I said.

'I'll pay you to wash the car.'

'No,' I repeated, in case they'd missed it the first time.

Dad threw his fork down. I imagine he did the same with his golf club when his ball disappeared into the trees, never to be seen again.

'You are going to stop those lessons now, do you hear me?' he shouted.

I leaped to my feet and clomped out of the room.

'Tyler, come back here.'

But I'd heard enough. Had enough. I went into the sitting room. There was Dexter in his basket, looking up at me expectantly, tongue lolling, eyes sparkling. At least someone was glad to see me.

'Come on, Dex, let's go.'

Our little family argument was clearly more appealing than the chilli con carne, because Mum and Dad followed me into the room. They sat on the sofa, but not close.

'Sit down.'

I stayed standing. As far away from them as I could.

'We're only thinking of you,' said Mum, fiddling with the cuff of her jumper. 'We don't want anything bad to happen to you. Why don't you join a summer camp?'

This had popped up several times in the build-up to the holidays. *Let's get rid of our annoying teenager for a few days so we can have the house to ourselves.*

'I won't know anyone.'

'What better way to solve that? Make new friends.'

I could see the logic in their argument, but right now logic was my number-one enemy. What I really wanted was revenge.

'I've already got friends. They're in London.'

'You've got to make an effort.'

'I'm teaching a girl to swim.'

Tick. Tock.

Shame they hadn't left that stupid clock behind in London.

Dad turned and glared at me. 'You can be a right pain sometimes.'

'Well, that makes three of us.'

Eight

• • • •

I found Mum sitting at the breakfast table, toying with a bowl of cereal. Dad had gone to work. Tallulah had gone to tennis camp. I made myself some toast with Marmite and sat at the furthest end of the kitchen table from her.

After a silence even I was starting to hate, Mum turned to me. 'Don't go to the pool today,' she said softly. I chomped my toast loudly. I know she hates that. 'Find something else to do.'

I could have made life so much easier for myself by uttering two little letters – 'O', 'K'. But decided not to. I'd had enough of being told what I could and couldn't do. I finished eating and put my plate in the sink.

'Plates don't clean themselves.'

'I'll clean it later.'

'Please.'

Please what? Please clean your plate. Please don't go to the lido. Please stop being an annoying little jerk.

What about pleasing me for a change? I ignored her and went into the utility to get my wetsuit.

Mum got up from the table and followed me. She stood in the doorway, arms folded, like a bouncer.

'I'm worried about you.'

I stuffed the wetsuit into my backpack.

'I want you to enjoy it up here, but you just won't make any effort. I'd like to see you mixing with kids your own age.'

I looked at the floor, the way you do when this sort of conversation turns up.

'There were lots of reasons why we came here.'

'But none of them included me.'

'They did include you. We want you to be safe.'

I looked out of the utility window. 'There are rocks up there I can fall off. Rivers I can drown in. Cows that can trample me.'

'You know what I'm talking about.'

Yes, London, with its gangs and muggers and drug dealers. None of which I ever came across in all my years living in Chiswick. Think Mum had got worse since she got the job watching stuff online. As if what she saw was going to happen to me.

'Just because you like it here, doesn't mean I have to.'

'You've got to make the most of things.'

'I am making the most of things. I'm going to the pool,' I said, grabbing my backpack.

'Please, find something else to do.'

No.

She was all out of arguments and finally stepped aside. I walked past her and out of the house.

Spider was already at the lido when I got there.

'Y'alreet?'

No. But I didn't want to bore her with the details of last night's happy family dinner, and Mum's moaning. It wasn't Spider's fault she wanted to learn to swim.

'Have you got my money?'

'I've got a fiver,' she said, taking it from her purse.

Why does nothing in my life ever run smoothly? I snatched the note from her. 'I want the rest next time. The money you owe me. You've no idea what I've been through to do this.'

'Well, let's put a bloody stop to it, then,' she said, snatching the money back.

Not what I expected. Or wanted.

I was about to lose my swimming money. Then what? Cleaning cars? Mowing lawns? Doing exactly what my mum and dad wanted.

I grabbed the money back.

'I'll teach you, Spider. But pay me what we agreed. I'm saving for some headphones. They're not cheap.'

She thought about it for a bit, then gave me the nod.

The lesson went worryingly well.

I got Spider to try floating on her back and kicking her legs, which I thought would prove impossible, but she mastered it quickly. Maybe Ilkley Lido was responsible, Spider desperate to learn as fast as possible to escape the clutches of the icy water. Not good. This was only lesson number three.

Afterwards we took up our usual position on the grass and tried to get our blood flowing. Spider was quieter than normal. The nervous look was back.

Thought I'd say something to cheer her up.

'Suppose you'll be off on your summer holidays soon.'

She picked at a blade of grass.

'I've gone away once. Not going away again.'

She didn't just speak Geordie. She spoke in riddles.

'What do you mean, gone away?'

She skipped my answer.

'Have yous gorra girlfriend?'

Shook my head. Hard enough finding two flaky male friends. God knows how long it would take to find an actual girlfriend.

'What about that lass over there?'

'What lass?'

'The one who keeps looking at you.'

Damn.

I'd got so into teaching Spider I'd forgotten to check the other people at the lido. On the far side, near the hedges, was Michele Hastings, a girl in my year, but a different class to me. She must have slipped in when I was in the pool with Spider. Now she'd spotted me and Spider. Probably texted half the school. *Seen Tyler Jackson with skinny white girl at the lido. Tell everyone you know.*

I wondered if she had her phone. 'Course she had her phone. She'd probably already taken a picture. *Look. Tyler Jackson's got his hand up the back of a girl. Tell everyone in Yorkshire.*

There was another reason for my anxiety. Michele is the type of girl I like stealing looks at. Medium height, slim, with hair that looks like she loves it, always nicely brushed and tied up with something. She's pretty, only slightly let down by one of those 'I know more than you do' expressions. On top of that, she was wearing a red bikini revealing a good fifty per cent more of her body than I was used to. I think I like her, but to be honest not enough words had passed between us to settle this one way or the other.

'D'ya know her?'

'A bit.'

'Well, why not know her a lot?'

Spider had a point. I'd spent months trying to find boys to hang out with, but totally ignored the other half of the population.

'Gan on, then,' urged Spider, elbowing me in the side.

'I'll speak to her next time.'

'Might not be a next time.'

Spider was right. I'd never seen Michele down the lido before. Might never see her here again. Also needed to know if she'd taken any pictures. I glanced in her direction. She gave me a little wave. I gave an even smaller one back and smiled even though I was too far away for it to mean anything. She was sitting with two other girls I didn't recognise. If they'd been from our year there was zero chance I'd go near them. I watched as her friends jumped into the lido, letting out horror film screams, leaving Michele alone on the grass.

'Now's your chance,' said Spider. 'Are you a man or a mouse?'

Actually, I'm a mouse, a boy mouse.

Come on, Tyler, get a grip.

I got slowly to my feet.

Despite the wetsuit, the cold water had done nothing to improve things in my swimming trunks department, so I wrapped my towel tightly around my waist, took a big breath and waddled my way across the grass towards Michele. As I got closer, my confidence got smaller. I'd probably said no more than half a dozen words to her, but now I was going to have to make whole sentences, maybe even paragraphs. And what on earth was I going to say? It was like the worst creative writing lesson ever, one where my brain has had everything of any interest erased.

I was no more than five metres away. It wasn't too late to veer off, and pretend I was going to the toilet. But before I had the chance to chicken out Michele turned towards me. 'Hi there, Tyler,' she said, in a twang that wasn't from round here.

'Oh, hi,' I said, trying to make it sound as though I'd just bumped into her, instead of homing in like a Michele-seeking missile. I needed to say something, something impressive, something that would make her like me.

'Hot today.'

'Do ya reckon?'

She clearly thought I was an idiot. It wasn't hot at all. I needed to get away from the weather. But before I could speak I suddenly realised just how much of Michele Hastings was on show. I've got quite an imagination when it comes to girls, but her bikini had made my imagination redundant. Wherever I looked there seemed to be flesh. She was so fit I had to look away.

'Haven't seen you here before,' I said, looking down at her tartan rug.

'That's because I hardly ever come here.'

Was she making fun of me, or just being polite?

'Sit down,' she said.

Wasn't sure how near to sit. Too close would make me seem a bit keen, too far would make it look as though I didn't like her, or she smelled. I split the difference. A metre seemed about right. I looked around to see if she had her phone out. Couldn't see one, but I knew it must be here somewhere.

'Have you got your phone?'

'Why? Do you need to call someone?'

'No, just wondered,' I said, realising how stupid this must sound.

''Course I have. It's in the locker.'

Result.

'Do you like swimming?'

'Hate it.'

Shame. It would have been great to teach Michele how to master the crawl.

'So how come you're down the lido?'

'My cousins wanted to come,' she said, nodding towards the two girls splashing each other in the shallow end. 'They're over from Sheffield.'

'Cool.' Though I'd never been to Sheffield and had no idea about its level of coolness. 'Where do you live?' I said, getting braver with my questions.

'Off Springs Lane, near the station.'

Not far.

'You're not from round here?'

'No, Manchester. Moved here couple of years ago.'

Couldn't believe it. I actually had something in common with her. Strangers in an alien county.

'So, who's your friend?' said Michele, looking over at Spider, who gave us a little wave.

'Someone I'm teaching to swim.'

'Didn't know you were a swimming instructor.'

I laughed nervously.

'Looks a bit old to be learning to swim.'

'A late starter.'

'Can't be at school. Not with that tattoo. Is she on holiday?'

'No.'

'She lives here?'

'Think so.'

Michele looked at me curiously. 'Do you make a habit of teaching strangers?'

'No, she just asked. She's paying me.'

'Things you do for money, eh?'

Was Michele having a go at me? Did she think I should have given the lessons for free? Did she think I was being stupid? Probably. Probably. And definitely.

'What's her name?'

'Lauren.'

'She's right skinny,' she said, looking over at her. Girls like to size each other up.

I hadn't come to talk to one girl and have her talk about another.

'Do you support Man United?'

'No,' she said, as though I'd asked the most stupid question ever.

'What's your favourite sport?'

'Running. Do you like it?'

'I can do it.'

'We should go for a run some time.'

'Cool.'

I was shocked at the speed of events. Two minutes ago I couldn't tell you a single thing about Michele. Now I knew all sorts of stuff. Spider would be proud of me.

'Tomorrow at ten, outside the Toy Museum,' she said.

'Tomorrow?'

'You busy?'

'No.' Even though I was. That's when I teach Spider.

I saw Michele's cousins getting out of the water. Time to head off. Couldn't face being grilled by three teenage girls in bikinis.

'Better get going.'

'Right, see you tomorrow, Tyler.'

I hurried away as fast as my towel skirt would allow, back to the spot where I'd been sitting.

Spider had gone.

Nine

●

●

I got changed as quick as I could and waited by reception. Spider must have changed even quicker, because there was no sign of her. Maybe she did have a job after all, or a college to go to somewhere. I was glad she'd made me go and speak to Michele but couldn't figure out why she hadn't waited. Needed to tell her I wouldn't be at the lido at our usual time. That was now impossible. I had no idea where she lived. Didn't even have her phone number.

Dilemma.

Do I ditch my run with Michele or my lesson with Spider? I could have gone back into the lido and changed the time with Michele. That would have been the sensible thing to do. But didn't want her to think I wasn't keen or, more importantly, that Spider was more important than she was. I'd give Spider her lesson another day. After all, she's got a season pass, so she's bound to be down the pool some other time.

There was another reason for my decision. I was more excited about Michele than I ever thought I would be. Over the last two terms I hadn't given her much brain time. No idea why. She was fit, lived in Ilkley, and as far as I knew didn't have a boyfriend. On top of that, I still had weeks of summer to get through. And last but not least, there was that red bikini.

I went home, my head sloshing around with inappropriate thoughts. Michele had made me totally forget what had gone on last night. But Mum hadn't.

'You went to the pool, didn't you?'

'Well spotted,' I said, as I took my wetsuit out of the bag, dropped it in the sink and began rinsing it under the tap.

Could sense she was right behind me.

'I don't like you talking to me like that.'

'I don't like the way you talk to me. As though I'm dumb.'

'I do not talk to you as though you're dumb. I'd never do that. I'm simply trying to reason with you.'

Silence.

'We care about you.'

Funny way of showing it.

I could hear Mum breathing behind me, as I ran cold water down the legs of the wetsuit.

'Look, I know things haven't gone the way you wanted here, but please try and make some sort of an effort. You're not the only one who had friends back in London. You've got to find new ones.'

Now would have been the perfect moment to tell her about Michele, but I didn't want to let her off the hook, so I carried on rinsing.

'Did you hear what I said?'

I mumbled a, 'Yeah.'

I imagined her face. Disappointment written in capital letters.

'How's this girl getting on with her lessons?'

'Okay.'

She put a hand on my shoulder. 'As soon as you've taught her to swim I want this to stop.'

Mum had given up trying to halt the lessons. You can win these battles if you're stubborn enough.

'Do you hear me?'

'Yes, Mum.'

She took her hand off my shoulder and walked away. For the first time this summer it seemed things were going well.

The following morning I woke up with an instant hit of guilt. I should have changed the time with Michele. Spider would be packing her bag, getting all excited, ready to head off to the lido. She'd get there and wonder where I'd gone. Probably think it was about the money, or lack of it. Assume I'd had enough of her. Then she'd head home, thinking that was the end of her swimming dream. She'd probably have a panic attack.

Felt as bad about Spider as I felt good about Michele.

Changed into my running gear and walked up to the Toy Museum. At ten o'clock on the dot Michele appeared around the corner, wearing only marginally more than she'd worn at the pool, a tight, body-hugging running vest, unbelievably short shorts, and bright red running shoes, with trainer socks. I had my old trainers on, football shorts and a T-shirt my gran had bought me with *I Love Scarborough* on the front.

'Hi, Tyler.'

'Hi,' I said.

Michele did some stretches against the railings, so thought I'd better do the same.

'Are you going on holiday?' she asked.

'I wish. Mum and Dad are saving for a new kitchen. Guess when it's fitted we'll turn the oven on, open the door and pretend we're somewhere hot.'

Michele laughed and touched my shoulder. It was only a touch but it sent a shiver on a lap of my body.

'What about you?'

'Going to Greece at the end of August.'

'Cool.'

'Not teaching your girl friend today?'

'She's not my girlfriend,' I snapped back, a little too quickly.

'There was a gap in there, Tyler – girl friend, not girlfriend.'

Felt stupid. But how was I meant to spot a space as minuscule as that?

Michele stopped stretching and checked her watch. 'Ready?'

'Yeah. How far we going?'

'Not far. About six k.'

Gulp.

If you put together all of my runs over the last year they wouldn't add up to that. But there was something even worse than the distance, the direction. There was a lovely bit of downhill road with our name on it, but what did Michele do – head up Wells Road towards the moors.

'Need to start off at a nice steady pace,' said Michele, who was going at Dexter-type speed. 'You should run so you can hold a conversation.'

At the current pace I was struggling to breathe, let alone talk. I'd walked up Wells Road many times, but the thought of running up it made no sense at all. People probably thought the same about me and swimming, up and down a freezing cold lido. But at least the pool is flat.

We finally reached the top, went through the gate and on to the path up to the moor.

'You must be pretty fit as a swimmer,' said Michele, talking as if she was sitting on a bus.

My words now had ridiculous gaps between them, gaps I had to fill with massive gulps of air.

'I ... guess ... but ... swimming's ... a ... different ... sort ... of ... fitness. It's ... all ... arms.'

'What about your legs?'

'Only ... a ... small ... amount ... of ... power ... comes ... from ... legs.'

I prayed that Michele had run out of questions.

'What's your mate Jack doing?'

I knew the answer to this one, but it would require a sentence. I chose a word instead.

'Dunno.'

'Do you have any brothers or sisters?'

Dunno wouldn't suffice here.

'Yes.'

Michele must have been wishing she'd met someone else at the lido, someone who could run and talk. I can do both, but not at the same time, not at this pace, not on this gradient. Why couldn't we have gone for a smoothie?

'What do you do apart from swim?'

Not wanting Michele to think I was a monosyllabic moron I somehow managed to string a sentence together. 'Can ... I ... tell ... you ... when ... we ... stop?'

She got the hint and stopped asking questions. But as a punishment for not speaking she upped the pace. Parts of my body that don't normally talk were now screaming, *What the hell do you think you're playing at?* To make matters worse, and matters were about as bad as matters get, I had Michele Hastings running alongside me, a girl from school. If it had been anyone else I'd have stopped, said I had a life-threatening stitch and walked home. But I couldn't let her think I was a loser. It would be all over social before you could say Snapchat.

We did half a dozen laps of Ilkley Tarn and then headed up the steep path towards the top. On and on we went. The moors above Ilkley are quite pretty as hills go, but today they'd turned into the ugliest torture chamber imaginable. Any thoughts of a sexual nature had been left miles behind. All I could think about was trying to stay alive.

We reached the wooden bridge over the boulder gorge and turned back. At last we were going downhill. The worst forty minutes of my life finally came to an end as we turned off the moor, past the big stone houses on Wells Road and came to a halt outside the Toy Museum.

'That was fun,' she panted.

If that was fun I'm a Vietnamese pot-bellied pig. Even my toughest reps in the pool couldn't compare to this, as I slumped on my knees, trying desperately to replace the oxygen she'd stolen from me. I went on all fours along the pavement and crawled up the railings, hugging them like a close relative.

'Look right knackered,' said Michele, her face a fetching shade of pink, bathed in the lightest sheen of sweat. I shuddered to think what my face looked like. It felt hot enough to need oven gloves.

I managed a nod.

'We should do that again some time.'

Doing that once in my lifetime was already once too many, but how could I say 'over my dead body'? She clearly loved this sort of crap.

'Maybe next summer,' I gasped.

She smiled. 'Okay, let's go to a café next time.'

Sitting down. *Oh, god, yes, please.*

'Saturday?'

I managed another nod.

'Here's my number,' she said, pulling a scrap of paper from her pocket. 'See you, Tyler.' And with that she ran off at an unnatural speed.

The meeting with Michele had gone both brilliantly and terribly. I'm not going to go over the terrible bit again, but what was brilliant was that Michele Hastings was keen enough to bring her phone number with her. The thought made me momentarily forget the lactic acid currently launching an all-out attack on my legs. I walked in slow motion through Ilkley, a smile super-glued to my face.

I reached the junction by All Saints Church and stopped at the lights. Over the road I spotted something a little out of the ordinary. Behind the multicoloured flower beds I saw someone lying on a wall. Not a sight you often see in the centre of Ilkley. The lights changed and I crossed the road. As I drew closer the person became more defined. She had her sleeves rolled up. One arm was covered in tattoos.

Ten

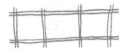

Spider was asleep on the wall.

Should I ignore her and carry on home? I still felt bad about ditching the swimming lesson this morning. But I wanted to know what she was doing here. Curiosity won.

'You okay, Spider?' I said, tapping her on the shoulder.

'Eh, what?' she grunted, rising from the depths of her sleep.

'It's me, Tyler.'

Spider smiled as her eyes brought me into focus. She sat up quickly, as if embarrassed to have been found lying down, like a kid in class caught slumped over their desk on a hot day. She looked dog-tired, eyes narrow, even though she had her glasses on.

'Where was you? Waited ages on the grass. Bloody ages.'

'Sorry. Went to see Michele, the girl at the pool, the one you made me see,' I said, trying to shove a bit of the blame in her direction. 'I wanted to tell you, but you'd gone.'

'It's alreet.' Even though her voice told me it wasn't.

'We can do the lesson tomorrow, normal time.'

Spider nodded, but looked sad, far sadder than you should be for just having missed a swimming lesson.

'And I've got the money I owe you.'

She fished in her pocket and pulled out a couple of five-pound notes. Then she delved deeper and pulled out a heap of coins.

'How much is it again?' she said, looking at the cash.

I'm crap at maths, unless it's about money I'm owed. She paid me two fivers, so that's three times seven-fifty, minus ten.

'Twelve-fifty.'

Spider scrabbled around with her money and got as far as ten pounds twenty-six pence.

'Reckon I've gorra few more coins hidden away somewhere,' she said, her hand diving further into her pocket. But from her expression the coins were nowhere to be found.

Felt sorry for me. Not getting paid enough.

But felt even sorrier for her.

'It's okay, Spider.'

I took the money from her and pocketed it. But it didn't make me happy, the way it should. It seemed like I'd cleaned Spider out.

I parked myself on the wall next to her.

'Is everything okay?'

She looked away, as if she hadn't heard me, or wanted to ignore me.

'Why were you lying on a wall?'

'Didn't sleep good last night. Needed to lie doon for a bit.'

I've felt tired loads of times, but never tired enough to sleep on a brick wall, right in the middle of town. If I was that shattered I'd go to bed.

'Any road, how's things with that lass? D'ya get anywhere with her?' she said, perking up.

'Yeah, right up there,' I said, looking up at the moors.

'Not what I meant, you wassack. Things must be belter. Your face has gan as red as a postbox.'

I didn't want to tell her how Michele had nearly killed me. I smiled instead.

'I'm happy for you, man, dead happy.'

Glad someone was pleased with something I'd done.

'Seein' her again, then?'

'Going to a café on Saturday.'

'Divvent gan to cafés, me. Too expensive.'

Spider looked miserable when she said that, even though it's just a café. Not like we were talking about a three-course meal at Betty's. It got me thinking about her. She never seemed to do anything. Never talked about her friends, her hobbies, her job. And now she was sleeping on a wall. I couldn't figure her out.

'Do you have any friends?'

Her face suddenly crumpled, as if my words had punched her. She bit her lip, trying to keep a cry inside. And then the old Spider came back.

'Aye, plenty,' she said, her voice cheery again. 'Plenty.'

'Where are they?'

Spider looked away as if trying to spot some of them.

'Oh, ye knaa, here and there, here and there.'

They might be there, but they certainly weren't here.

'Bet you've got plenty back in Tyneside.'

'Aye,' she said, but the word came out flat, as though she didn't mean it.

'Do you have any friends in Ilkley?'

'Just the one.'

Then she looked at me.

Could that be true? Me, Tyler Jackson, her only friend in Ilkley? Where were all her other mates? Wasn't as though she was horrible. Or boring. Thought the older you got the more friends you got. Unless you're really old and they're all dead. Maybe she was fussy about who she hung out with. Or maybe she'd done something bad and scared them all off. Or maybe, like me, she'd been dragged far from home, her friends left in her wake, finding it hard to make new ones.

I touched her back with my hand, like I'd done in the lido. Briefly. Felt she needed it.

Spider gave me one of her widest smiles. I took my hand back and looked at her. She seemed skinnier than normal. I know for a fact girls don't like to put on weight. Mum's terrified of our scales. But Spider was at the other end. She looked as though she could do with a good feed. I hopped off the wall.

'Y'off home?'

'Not yet.'

I crossed the road and went to a shop. I came back with a Mars bar, and offered it to her. She resisted, for about a second.

'You're a star.'

She wolfed it down and ate the crumbs out of the wrapper.

I felt worried for her.

'Do you not have a summer job?'

'Not any more.'

No wonder she struggled to pay for her lessons. No wonder she could only get one arm tattooed.

She got up from the wall stiffly. 'I'd berra be off. Are we meeting at the pool the morrow?'

'Sure.'

And she walked away, like someone in no hurry to get anywhere.

She was a strange one, that's for sure.

Eleven

I went home, had a shower and made myself a fried-egg sandwich. Still wasn't sure whether to tell Mum about Michele. I could never figure out what her reaction might be, like in chemistry when you mix chemicals together not knowing if there's going to be an explosion or not.

Decided to take the risk.

'Michele?' she said, with a rare full-on grin.

'Yeah, she's in my year.'

'And what's she like?'

The image of Michele in her red bikini popped into my inbox. I decided not to describe it.

'Er, she's okay.'

'Okay? That the best you can come up with?'

'Got nice hair.'

Mum laughed. 'Well, that's a start. But what's she like as a person?' Mum's into that sort of thing. She watches programmes where people talk about each other. No action. No special effects. Just talk.

'Seems nice.'

'Where did you meet?'

'In town.'

Didn't want to spoil things by mentioning the lido.

'I'm happy for you.'

I was pleased Mum was pleased. Made a change from arguing. Guess she hoped Michele would stop me moaning about Ilkley. That she'd help me settle down. Give me someone to hang out with over the summer, apart from an eighteen-year-old Geordie who couldn't swim.

I met Spider at the normal time. She wasn't her usual self. Seemed twitchy, as if she'd done something wrong. I decided not to mention the talk we'd had on the wall. Got the feeling it wouldn't make the situation better. Mum says you need to get things out in the open. But sometimes it's best to lock your words away.

The lesson didn't go well. Which was good for me, but bad for her. I tried to get her to hold the float with one hand and swim with the other, but she was useless at it, and kept falling off, swallowing half the lido.

'Keep this up and they'll need to refill the pool.'

But Spider didn't laugh.

'Can we get out now, Tyler? I've had enough.'

We'd only done fifteen minutes. Three pounds seventy-five pence worth of lesson. I was never going to get rich at this rate. But I could tell she wasn't interested.

We went over to the grass and got our blood flowing again.

'Do you still want to carry on the lessons?' I said, fearing for my headphones.

A tiny nod of her head.

'Wanna keep gannin. Not in the mood today.'

Spider looked even more fed up than she'd been on the wall.

'Is everything all right at home?'

Spider squeezed her towel tight around her legs as her head slumped forwards. She stayed slumped for some time.

'Did I say something wrong?'

Spider's head surfaced from the towel. 'Na.'

Not used to situations like this.

'Anything I can do to help?'

She snorted a laugh. 'Don't happen to have a spare house, do you?'

Confused.

She moved her hand over the 'Mam' tattoo, as close to crying as you can get without getting around to it.

'What do you mean, "spare house"?'

'Nowt. Just ignore me. Daft words from a daft Geordie.'

'You've got a house…'

'That's enough,' shouted Spider.

She wouldn't tell me what she did, why she was here,

why she got so moody. We were soon going to run out of things to talk about.

'Still want a lesson tomorrow?'

'Aye, still want me lessons. Not giving up that easily. See yous the morrow.'

And with that she gathered up her stuff and hurried off to the changing rooms.

Why couldn't I find someone normal to teach?

After the strange morning with Spider, I met Michele. She'd texted me to say where – a little café off the high street. Though I noticed there was one tiny letter missing from the end of her text – 'x'.

Got to the café first and grabbed a table. She was eighteen minutes, thirty-six seconds late. I got to my feet, wondering if she'd give me a hug or at least an apology. But nothing. She sat straight down.

'Hi, Michele,' I said, cheerily as I could.

'Hello,' she said, the way you would to someone in class you've got zero interest in.

She sat, head down, preferring to look at her phone than at me. Couldn't figure out why she was hacked off. The silence rumbled on. How typical was that? She wants to talk when we're sprinting like cheetahs, but when we're sitting still she won't say a word. I'd never been on a date before, but I knew that silences weren't good, unless it's because your mouth's full of someone else's tongue.

'What would you like?' I said.

'Strawberry smoothie.'

Not thanks, please, great. Just her order.

I bought two smoothies and sat opposite the stony-faced Michele. She took a long, noisy slurp, put her phone down and looked me dead in the eyes. 'What's going on with you and that girl down the lido?'

Grumpy face explained.

'Nothing,' I said, the word coming out high-pitched.

'You were with her at All Saints.'

'You followed me?'

'No, Nat Swan saw you. She texted me.'

Ilkley was way too small.

'Was just talking.'

'I don't want to be pissed around, Tyler.'

'Honest, we were talking.'

'Nat said you had your arm around her.'

'I touched her back.'

'Why?'

'I, I … felt sorry for her.'

'Why?'

'She seemed upset.'

'About her swimming lessons?'

'No, just life, I guess.'

'How come you met her in town?'

'I didn't meet her. I bumped into her. Didn't know she was gonna be there.'

Now it was my turn to take a long slurp. Was Michele jealous of me just for touching another girl's back? Maybe that was all it took.

'I'm trying to help her to swim. She gets panic attacks.'

Michele laughed dismissively. 'Oh, yeah, Mia Thompson gets those ... when she's not getting enough attention.'

'She *does* get panic attacks.'

'You've seen them?'

'Not yet.'

'Bet it'll be some pathetic squirmy thing,' she said, waving her arms as though there was a wasp nearby. 'That's what Mia does.'

'Only saying what she told me. I'm not going out with her.'

'Never said you were.'

But you thought it.

Michele had made me feel guilty about something I had no reason to feel guilty about. It was like being at home.

'Why isn't someone at the lido teaching her to swim?'

I came here to get to know Michele better and all we'd done was talk about Spider.

'What do you like doing, Michele, apart from running?'

'I haven't finished yet. Why doesn't someone else teach her?'

Exhale.

'How should I know? Maybe she likes me.' Wrong answer, Tyler, completely wrong answer. 'Or maybe she doesn't.'

Michele leaned over the table. 'My mum gave me one piece of advice. Don't ever let men, or, in your case, boys, mess you around.'

'Why would I do that?'

'Mum says it's in the male DNA.'

Michele's mum had clearly been through something bad. I suppose that was my fault as well.

'I am *not* going out with her.'

A wicked smile crossed Michele's face.

'Prove it.'

'How?'

'By stopping these stupid lessons.'

Twelve

'Girls are beyond weird, Dexter. Don't go near them.'

But Dexter wasn't interested. He only had one thing on his mind. Sticks. I searched the ground for a suitable projectile and threw it as far as I could. The boomerang dog brought it back.

'Just wanted to meet Michele, find out a bit more about her, and it ends with her saying I've got to stop seeing Spider. How the hell did that happen?'

Dexter had no idea.

'I need a new pair of headphones. Then I won't have to listen to anyone.'

I threw a big stick, more of a log, really, but Dexter somehow managed to haul it back.

'Should have put my foot down and said no. Do that to Mum and Dad all the time, why didn't I do that to her? Sorry, Dex, not a fair question. You haven't seen Michele in a bikini.'

Dexter went sniffing through the grass.

'Wish I was better at talking, like the people in Mum's TV dramas. They always come out with something clever. I didn't manage anything. Just sat staring at her.'

Michele had got me with that face, and that shiny hair, and that body. When you've got your horny head on, it's impossible to talk properly. I was like that in French with Miss Dubois. I quite like French, but my eyes like her even more. That's why I got a four.

Dexter saw a bird and chased it. The bird flew off and Dexter came back, his tongue dangling like a big piece of bacon.

'What am I going to do about Spider? Can't let her down.'

Dexter panted. I think he agreed with me.

It seemed nobody wanted me to teach Spider to swim, apart from Spider. Even though I fancied Michele, I couldn't let her tell me what to do. We weren't even going out. On top of that I felt sorry for Spider. She seemed so … lost. And she needed to stop her panic attacks. Not bad reasons to keep meeting someone.

Decided to meet Spider at our usual time. Didn't think there was much chance Michele would be around, but her spies could be out, sending photos, texting. *He's holding her hands and pulling her through the water. Like they're on holiday.* But I had a plan of my own. For future lessons I'd ask Spider to get there at eight o'clock. Most people tended to arrive later, when the sun's higher and the water marginally less frozen. With any luck my lesson would be over before any girls from our year turned up.

Ten a.m.. Ilkley Lido.

'You look a bit nervous, Tyler.'

That makes two of us.

We flashed our season passes and went in. The lido was quiet. Today's temperature had so far fought and failed to get into the teens, but Spider was already in the pool when I came out of the changing rooms, holding the side and kicking her legs furiously. I admired her guts. Someone willingly getting into cold water with a teenager who until recently had never ever given a swimming lesson. Either very brave. Or very stupid.

Seeing as Spider seemed more confident today, I thought I'd try and get her moving under her own steam.

'What I want you to do is move to the wall.'

'Walking?'

'No, swimming.'

I didn't think she'd be able to manage, but it would be a good way of seeing how far she'd come.

'Blow bubbles out underwater as I taught you, kick

your legs like you've been doing, and move your arms like this,' I said, doing crawl strokes in the air.

'Here we gan.'

Spider moved a few steps back, took a gigantic breath and hurled herself at the wall. It was more thrashing than swimming. The sort you see in a film when someone's drowning. She surfaced, well short of her destination, coughing and spluttering.

'Forgot to close me mouth,' she said, gulping air.

'Give it another go. But this time try to take it slower. It's not a race.'

Having recovered, Spider took a series of deep gulps and dived forward, her arms and legs moving in a peculiar manner. It wasn't like any swimming stroke I'd ever seen but she somehow reached the wall. She stood up, beaming. From her face you'd think she'd won the Olympic Gold medal.

'I did it, Tyler,' she screamed. 'I bloody did it.'

'Yes, you did,' I said, smiling.

She waded through the water and squeezed me hard, as though I was a tube of toothpaste with the tiniest bit left inside. I prayed none of Michele's friends were about.

'Yer a friggin genius, Tyler. Let me gan again.'

And sure enough, Spider did. It wasn't pretty, it wasn't far, but she was moving through the water under her own speed, which is technically swimming.

'I'm deein it, man,' she gasped.

I was happy and sad in equal measure. Happy I'd managed to teach someone to swim. Sad to see my headphones disappearing into the depths.

'You just need to keep practising now.'

'Na, I need yous to teach me to dee it proper, like. I wanna gan up and doon the pool like a speedboat.'

I'd have left school by the time Spider could do that. But I admired her ambition.

'Try getting used to being underwater. Take a big breath and just use your legs.'

'Do me best,' she said, smiling.

Spider inflated her skinny chest and dived below the surface. As she did her submarine impression, I noticed a squat woman wearing gym leggings and a T-shirt come storming into the lido. She had no swim bag or picnic, but what she did have was a red face and two clenched fists.

'Where the bloody hell is she?' she screamed, looking around. The woman was also a Geordie.

Something told me the person she wanted was now torpedoing below the surface.

'I knaa you're in here, you bastard.'

Spider finally broke the surface, spluttering.

'You cow,' screamed the woman as she spotted Spider and came storming over to the edge of the pool, fists still balled tight.

Spider took off her goggles, squinting to bring the woman into focus. 'Chrissie,' she said, a terrified look on her face.

'You've gorra bloody cheek. Using me pass. Wearing me bloody swimming costume. Never said yous could have that.'

'Just borrowed it.'

'What? Like you borrowed me money?' screamed Chrissie.

The few people in the lido stopped what they were doing to watch the commotion, apart from a guy in the swimming section with earplugs in, who carried on crawling up and down the pool, oblivious to the drama.

A female lifeguard in a blue uniform came down from her high chair and walked over to the woman. 'Can you calm down, please?' she said.

But Chrissie looked beyond calming.

'I'm not friggin' gannin anywhere till I find out what she's done with me bloody money.'

'Said I'll pay yous back,' said Spider, desperation in her voice.

'Gonna rob a bank, are yous?'

'I'll gerrit.'

'Fifty quid, you've taken. Fifty, that I knaa of. I'm sick of yous, d'ya here me? Sick. You are oot, today, and you're not coming back.'

But she wasn't finished. She leaned over and gobbed on Spider.

'Oi, no spitting in the pool,' shouted the lifeguard.

Chrissie didn't care. She turned and stormed out of the lido.

I stared at Spider, dumbstruck.

'What was all that about?'

Spider said nothing. Her breathing grew faster and faster as though she'd been swimming lengths all morning. Her face was as white as an envelope. She looked frightened and wrapped her thin arms tight round her floppy costume.

'Me chest. I cannit breathe,' she said, gasping.

'You okay, Spider?'

She shook her head.

'Feel dizzy. Feel hot.'

How could you possibly feel hot in Ilkley Lido?

She put her hand to her head, then her eyes closed and no more words were uttered. Spider fell backwards and slipped beneath the water.

Thirteen

Lifeguards leaped into the pool and lifted Spider out. They carried her limp, dripping body to the grass and laid her down on a towel.

'Stand back,' they said, as a small crowd of gawpers formed.

People love an incident.

The lifeguards checked her breathing and her pulse. From the looks on their faces they weren't as panicked as Spider.

'Is she a friend of yours?' said one of them, turning to me.

'Sort of. I was helping her to swim.'

'Yeah, I've been watching you,' she said. 'You should leave that to the experts.'

So everyone keeps saying.

'Wasn't my fault,' I said, in a quaky voice. I didn't want the police involved. Or worse still, Mum or Dad.

'It's okay,' said another lifeguard, kneeling over

Spider. 'We saw what happened. Seems like the lass fainted.'

A few seconds later Spider came around and turned her screwed-up eyes on the faces peering down at her. She looked terrified, until she spotted me.

'Tyler.'

'It's okay, Spider.'

She tried to get up, but with a gentle hand a lifeguard eased her back down.

'Take it slowly,' she said. 'What happened to you, love?'

'Had a funny turn.'

Nothing funny about it to me. The way her breathing had gone out of control, the look of terror on her face, followed by the blackout.

Someone brought a chair. They lifted Spider into it and wrapped her in another towel. She sat there for a while, taking in big breaths, until the faintest hint of colour came to her face.

'Y'okay to go inside?' asked a lifeguard.

Spider nodded.

They got her to her feet and, with an arm round two of the lifeguards, she took tiny shuffly steps into a little office at the back of reception.

Was so glad there'd been no one from school to witness this. I would be trending at number one: #Tylernearlydrownsgirl. They found a chair for Spider and someone brought her a big mug of steaming tea.

The mug made me smile. It had a slogan on the side: *The World's Best Swimmer.*

They checked her pulse again, and one of the lifeguards looked into her eyes. They seemed happier now.

'Feeling better, love?'

Spider nodded. But she still had that horrified look on her face.

'Has someone got me glasses?'

They'd brought her bag in. I fished inside and found them.

'Thanks,' she said, taking them from me and popping them on. She looked like Spider again.

'You need to get yourself checked by your doctor. Have you got a doctor in Ilkley?' asked the female lifeguard.

Spider nodded. But something about her nod told me she didn't.

'We'll leave you two here for a bit,' she said.

Wouldn't look good if someone drowned at the lido because all the lifeguards were looking after a girl who hadn't drowned.

They left. It was just me, Spider and the steaming mug of tea. I grabbed a chair and sat opposite her.

'What was all that about?'

'Had a funny turn.'

'I mean before that. The woman, Chrissie.'

Spider could sometimes be bubbly, but it was as

though all of her bubbles had been burst. Her face couldn't have looked more downbeat. A droplet slid down her face, but it was just pool water.

I didn't want to keep on at her, but I needed to know. 'Speak to me, Spider.'

She put her tea down on a table and squeezed both hands tight.

'Chrissie's me cousin. Been staying with her.'

'And you took her money, and her pass, and her swimming costume?'

'Borrowed the pass, and her cossie. Never saw her use them.'

'What about the money? That's why you didn't pay me, isn't it? You never had any money, did you?'

'I did have money,' she said, her voice cracking. 'And I told her I'd pay her back. Was only a few quid.'

Fifty, if I remember rightly. Lot more than a few.

'I'll pay her back,' she repeated.

Spider went for her tea and took a slurp.

'Your cousin said she wants you out. Out of where?'

Spider had that stare on her face, the one she wore when she was on the church wall, and when she looked up at the moor. Thought maybe she hadn't heard me. But she had all right. Her face began to crumple. I saw another drop fall, but this time the water wasn't from the pool. Two rivulets of tears were now coursing down her cheeks.

'What's the matter, Spider?'

But she couldn't speak. Her whole body rocked back and forth as though some internal earthquake was going on. Great big sobs broke from her lips. She hunched over and grabbed her bony knees, the tears filling up the insides of her glasses.

Didn't know what to do. I'd only wanted to earn a few quid to get some headphones. I thought of calling Mum. But she didn't even want me here. She'd have her told-you-so face on. *You should never have got involved, Tyler. Should have left it to the experts.*

But who are the experts at things like this? When someone you don't know very well starts crying and won't tell you why. How do you help someone like that? I wanted to go, but there was no one else here for her. What had she said, I was her only friend in Ilkley? There had to be someone else. But where were they? I got up and put a hand on her damp shoulder.

'It's okay.'

Spider wiped her wet glasses on her towel. 'No, it's bloody not okay,' she sobbed. 'I haven't got a home to go to.'

'What do you mean?'

'Chrissie wants me out of her house. I've got no one. I've got nowhere.'

That's impossible. Everyone's got someone, somewhere. She must be exaggerating. Maybe Michele was right about her. Just a drama queen, looking for sympathy to get her own way.

'What about your relatives? You must have other relatives.'

Spider gripped the word 'Mam' on her arm, as though she never wanted to let go. She looked up from the tattoo and stared at me, her face desperate, spit on her lips. 'You just divvent gerrit, do yous, Tyler?'

No, not a word of it.

'I'm not like you. I haven't got me own room. Haven't got a bed. I haven't got a mam and dad who want me home every night. I haven't got anything.'

'Why not?'

'I just haven't,' she shouted.

Tears once again began to make their way down her cheeks. I was wrong about her being a drama queen. You can't make up tears. Not that many.

'Thought I was gonna gerrit sorted this time. Thought I'd found somewhere to make a new start. I've blown it. Bloody back to square one.'

She hugged her knees again.

I came up with the only bit of advice I could think of.

'Why not go back to your cousin? Tell her you're sorry about the money. Tell her you'll pay her back. That's a good idea, isn't it?'

From the expression on Spider's face it was the worst idea ever.

'You don't know Chrissie. Or her boyfriend.'

'What's he got to do with it?'

Spider wiped her glasses on the towel and put them back on again.

'It's his flat.'

Spider was his lodger. Starting to make sense.

'Sofa surfing, heard of that?'

Shook my head.

'Sounds fun, doesn't it, surfing on a sofa, like you're in Hawaii or somewhere? But it's not. It's a bloody nightmare. I've got no bedroom. Spend every night on their settee. Can't sleep when I want. Can't get up when I want. Can't stay as long as I want. That's my world, Tyler.'

Kipping on other people's sofas. Doesn't sound bad, for a night or two maybe, like a sleepover. But nobody wants a sleepover to go on for ever. The sitting room will start to smell. And people will want their sofa back. They'll want to watch TV. And then what?

'Have you been thrown out before?'

Spider did a big sniff. 'Aye, a few times.'

'Where did you go?'

'Where do you think I went? The streets.'

'The streets?'

'The actual bloody streets.'

Couldn't believe what I was hearing. I thought people who slept on the streets were older men with beards and scruffy jackets, not eighteen-year-old girls.

'Was dead scary, especially at night. Met this lass. We used to wander round and kip during the day.'

'Why didn't you tell me you were homeless?'

Spider wiped tears from her face.

'Not something you boast aboot.'

I had no idea what to say or do. All that was missing was the gold clock from our mantelpiece. The only sound came from kids squealing as warm bodies met cold water.

Big breath.

'I've got to go, Spider,' I said, getting to my feet. 'Are you gonna be all right?'

She laughed, a bitter little laugh.

'Go and see Chrissie and sort it out. Then let's meet at the lido tomorrow. Eight o'clock.'

'I've got no bloody money.'

Nearly mentioned the fifty quid. Thought better of it.

'You can have this one for free.'

Spider gave a smile that was so small it almost wasn't.

I took it as a yes, although it could equally have been a no.

I had to go. I couldn't stand this. I couldn't solve this. I put a hand on Spider's arm.

'See you tomorrow.'

Fourteen

'That was a bad morning.'

Dexter didn't disagree with me, as we walked across Riverside Gardens to the bridge. Wondered what Spider was doing now. Hoped she'd taken my advice and asked her cousin Chrissie for forgiveness. Although someone who screams at you and gobs on your head doesn't seem the forgiving type. But you can't stay angry for ever, can you? My mum tries, but even she gets tired of it and gives up.

Then a bad thought took root. What if Chrissie and her boyfriend really had had enough of Spider and wanted their sofa back. Where would she go? I still couldn't believe she had no one to help her. She's not that old, so she must have grans and grandads somewhere. If they were anything like my grandparents in Derby they'd do anything for her. If I turned up at their door and said Mum and Dad had thrown me out for not loving Yorkshire enough, they'd let me stay as long as I liked.

Maybe Spider wasn't telling me the whole truth. What if she'd done something really terrible on Tyneside, something so bad no one would want her back, not even for the night? Maybe that's why nobody wanted her around. But she didn't seem like a drug dealer or a thief to me. Just a girl who wanted to learn to swim.

The problem with Spider was that she never opened up about what had gone on, as if the memories were too painful or too big to dig up. Who knows? I thought maybe I should tell Mum what had happened. The thought was quickly snuffed out. I'd never hear the last of it.

She could have drowned. That's precisely why you should never have been giving lessons in the first place. Why didn't you listen to us? You could have killed her.

But I could tell her something.

Knock. Knock.

'Mum?'

'Just a second.'

We weren't allowed to go in the study when she was working, in case we saw something that would give us nightmares until the day we died.

'Come in.'

Went in. Mum was sitting at her desk, laptop off. She looked as if she'd been up all night watching horror movies.

'Y'okay, Mum?'

'I'll be all right shortly. What is it?'

'I'm stopping the swimming lessons.'

I'd decided to give Spider one more lesson, so they were as good as over.

A smile briefly lightened her face. 'What's brought this about?'

'Been thinking about what you and Dad said. It's the right thing to do.'

'Really?'

'Yeah, really.'

I agree with Mum and Dad about once every three years. I could tell from her eyes how momentous this was.

'Well, that's great news. But what about this girl you've been teaching?'

'I got her to swim ten metres. Guess she can find someone else to teach her to swim the rest of the length.'

'She okay about that?'

'Yeah, pretty cool.'

Mum got up from her chair and gave me a hug.

I gave her a little squeeze back. She looked like she needed one.

'Your dad will be pleased. Now, are you going to go for those other summer jobs?'

'I guess.'

For the first time since I won the school swimming race Mum looked proud of me.

Next day I rode my bike to the lido, chained it to the fence and waited for Spider. And waited and waited and waited. Eight o'clock became nine o'clock. It looked like she'd had enough of swimming lessons. Maybe she was happy to get her ten-metre badge. Or maybe she'd forgotten about the new time.

The sun had already punched its way through the early morning clouds and was beaming down on Ilkley. The radio said it was going to reach twenty-six degrees today. Typical. The one day I'm not swimming is the day it's going to be boiling. Spider might have actually lasted the full half-hour.

Part of me was glad she hadn't turned up. Hot weather never failed to bring hordes to the lido. Among them were bound to be some Year Tens, soon to be Year Elevens. They'd spot me and Spider and, in the blink of a smartphone, Michele Hastings would know.

I continued to watch people troop in, laden with picnic bags and blankets, ready to spend a day on the grass, with the occasional quick dip in icy water, before heading home with wet bathers and sunburn.

Where was she?

Spider had always been pretty reliable when it came to meeting, but not today.

I hate waiting, even when I've got nothing better to do than wait. I hung around until ten-thirty and decided to call it a day.

I needed to talk to someone about what had gone on. There was only one candidate, one human candidate.

Michele.

I texted her and we arranged to meet in the park by the river. This time she was only ten minutes late. I hoped she'd forgiven me for putting a hand on Spider's back.

'Hi, Michele.'

'Hi,' she said, with something that could almost pass for enthusiasm.

We sat on the swings, gently rocking to and fro. But, having arranged to meet, I began to have doubts about telling her what had happened. She'd given me strict instructions not to give any more swimming lessons to Spider. And what had I done? Just that. The story wouldn't really work in any other setting, though. I could hardly say she'd had a panic attack in the Co-op over the price of yoghurts.

'Michele.'

'Yes.'

'I gave another lesson to that Geordie girl.'

'Lauren?'

Forgot I'd called her that.

'Yeah, her.'

She scraped the bottom of her sandals along the ground and brought the swing to a sudden halt. 'I said you had to stop.'

'I owed her a last lesson. It's over now.'

'You've definitely stopped?'

'Definitely. Totally.' I sneaked a peek at her legs before continuing the story. 'But something strange happened.'

'She learned to swim?'

'No, her cousin turned up at the lido, went mental, said she'd taken money from her and was throwing her out of the house.'

'Good.'

Not quite what I was expecting.

'What's good about it?'

'Well, if Lauren was stealing she deserves to be chucked out. Sounds like a total nightmare.'

'Says she's got nowhere to live.'

'Attention-seeking again. 'Course she's got somewhere to live.'

'But what if she really has got nowhere to go?'

'Don't be stupid. If she's lost her home, there are hostels and places. She's taking you for a ride.'

'You don't know her, Michele.'

'And how long have *you* known her? A couple of weeks? Suppose you'll be doing Lauren for GCSE?'

Michele seemed happy with her little quip. But I was angry inside. I wanted her to believe me, but I only had Spider's word for it. I didn't have proof. I kicked my legs back and forth.

'She *did* have a panic attack.'

'I bet she cried as well.'

Nodded.

'Yeah, typical attention-seeker, turning on the tears like a tap. She's caught you, hook, line and sinker,' said Michele, reeling in the line of an imaginary fishing rod.

Michele had left me feeling annoyed and stupid. I'd wanted to talk about someone who needed help, but she'd twisted it so that I was the one who needed help. Not sure how that had happened. I was looking for advice, maybe a bit of support. Instead I got an ear-bashing. Hadn't even got around to talking about how I could help Spider. Maybe it was jealousy, or anger, or insecurity – or all three. How should I know? Stuff like this always baffles me.

'Don't get caught like that, Tyler. You've got to stand up for yourself. That's why I've just dumped Luke Garrard, from Year Eleven.'

Nearly fell off the swing. Michele was a factory, churning out surprises.

'Didn't know you were seeing anyone.'

'Went out for a bit, but discovered he's mad for Sadie Hetherby. Finished it by text.'

'Text? Why didn't you tell him?'

''Cos he's on holiday. Said it wasn't working, *blah, blah, blah.*'

'You actually wrote *blah, blah, blah*?'

'Yeah. And I mentioned you.' Swallowed what little spit I could find. 'Said I've been hanging out with Tyler Jackson.'

'You used my full name?'

Michele nodded.

This was the nightmare that carries on after you've woken up.

'He'll think we're going out.'

'He might,' said Michele. 'Don't really care.'

'And when's he back from holiday?'

'Soon.' Michele looked at me. 'You've gone a bit pale, Tyler.'

Fifteen

It was time to move on from Spider. I'd enjoyed being with her. Felt pleased I'd taught her to swim, sort of. She'd filled a hole in my holidays where friends should have been. She'd earned me one-tenth of a headphone. But I realised her problems were way too big for me to solve. She needed a house to stay in, another sofa to sleep on, money to buy stuff. Three things I didn't have. Sometimes feeling sad for people is all you can do.

On top of that, I had something new to worry about. Luke Garrard.

I'd tried to get more information from Michele, but she'd stayed tight-lipped. My imagination filled in the gaps she'd left. Luke had been mad for Sadie, but what had he done to deserve being dumped? Maybe he'd been giving her private swimming lessons? Or perhaps he'd been seen touching Sadie's back? And what was Luke like? I pictured him as a rugby player, whose idea of fun was bench-pressing massive weights and laying into a punch bag. I didn't want to be that punch bag.

'Maybe we should just run away, Dex?'

I think he'd have liked this. Up to the point when he needed dog food.

I'd had high hopes for Michele, but apart from both being removed from the city where we were born and going to the same school we didn't have an awful lot in common. I still wasn't one hundred per cent sure why she wanted to go out with me. *Hanging out with, Tyler.* Weren't those her words? There's a canyon-sized gap between hanging out and going out. Maybe she wanted to test me, see if I was boyfriend material, and that I wouldn't cheat on her. But I still had no idea what my marks were. I'd kept up with her on the run. I'd bought her a smoothie. I hadn't bragged about her on Instagram. Was that a pass or a fail?

See you soon.

Those were her last words.

'Maybe the worst is over, Dex. Maybe with Spider gone, and Luke finished with, and Michele with no one left to hate, things will get better.'

Dexter didn't seem that bothered either way and ran after a bird he had no chance of catching.

After a long walk through the river valley we headed home. We were approaching The Moody Cow, when

I suddenly stopped dead in my tracks. Up ahead was Spider's cousin, Chrissie, weighed down with two bulging plastic carrier bags. The sight of her brought the pool incident gushing back. The spitting. The shouting. The swearing. Spider's confession.

I could feel my heart pounding in my ears, like I'd dived too deep.

Felt a bit sick, thinking what it must be like to be thrown out by the very people who are meant to be helping you. I knew that would never happen to me, not in a billion years. Even though I row with Mum and Dad, I know they love me, and wouldn't want me to come to any harm. But what about Spider? Had she really run out of relatives? Did her cousin honestly not care one jot what happened to her? Wasn't there anyone who loved her enough to give her a sofa?

I began to follow Chrissie.

'It's okay, Dex. Going for a slightly longer walk today. Need to find out what happened to my swimming pupil. The one no one likes.'

Dexter seemed happy with this. As long as it involved walking.

'She had a panic attack. Dogs probably don't get those. But humans do. Saw Spider have one, a real one. Not good.'

We slowed our pace to make sure we didn't catch Chrissie up.

'Want to make sure she's okay.'

We followed Chrissie past the station, up Wheatley Road and down Clifton Road. Then Dex and I stopped as we saw her put her bags down and open a gate. A few seconds later she had her key out and was inside.

'What now, Dex?'

He looked up at me with eyes that said, *You're the human, you work it out.*

I was scared to speak to her. I'd seen how mad Chrissie had been at the pool. Maybe she'd be mad with me. Might spit in my face. But how else would I find out what had happened to Spider? I opened the gate, tied Dexter to a wheelie bin in the front garden and walked down the path. My breathing was shallow, mouth dry, heart misbehaving. I stopped at the front step. It was like the moment before you jump into Ilkley Lido.

Come on, Tyler, it's only a house.

Deep breath.

Rapped on the door with the knocker.

Hadn't felt this nervous since a couple of hours ago, when Michele told me about Luke. I heard footsteps in the hallway. A second later the door opened to reveal a blank-faced Chrissie.

'What?'

Don't think Chrissie recognised me. Must have been concentrating so hard on giving Spider a bollocking she'd paid no attention to the boy in the wetsuit.

'I-I'm Tyler. I was giving Spider swimming lessons.'

Chrissie filled in her blank face with a look of sheer venom. 'After bloody money, is that what it is?'

From what I'd seen at the pool, should have guessed what Chrissie's reaction would be. Needed to think of something. Quick.

'I've got some money from Spider to give you.'

This seemed to knock the wind out of her sails. She blew out air. Hers was cigarette flavoured.

'Berra come in.' She spotted Dexter. 'That bastard berra not crap in me garden.'

I went inside and Chrissie closed the door. She lived in half a house. The people next door must live upstairs. This house lived downstairs. I followed her along a corridor into a small sitting room. If Chrissie had money, she didn't spend much of it on her house. The carpet was frayed and the furniture seemed ready for the charity shop. The only thing that looked modern was the enormous TV in the corner. Never been in a house like this before.

Chrissie's hands disappeared into the sleeves of her sweatshirt. It was the first time I'd got a good look at her. She had a nice face, not dissimilar to her cousin's. The rest of her was the opposite of Spider, short, stocky and glasses-free.

'Sit doon.'

She sounded the spit of Spider.

I sat on her sofa and ended up with my knees in line with my head. Some big bums had clearly hollowed this out, like glaciers gouging a valley.

Chrissie sat on a little footstool.

'Is this where Spider slept?'

Nodded.

'When I heard what she was gannin through, said she could stay here.'

Thought Spider was joking about that sofa surfing stuff, but it was true. This was her home, a lumpy, stained, battered old sofa. No wonder she'd been sleeping on the wall in town. No one could get a decent kip on this thing.

'Wor Spider came here a couple of months back.'

'What was happening back home?'

'Dad's a total bastard. One thing I know she's not lying aboot. Stayed with a few people in Newcastle. Said she was running out of sofas. Asked if she could stay with me. I got her a cleanin' job. Was alreet for a bit. But she started taking stuff. Or borrowing, as she calls it. Couldn't even pay the rent she owed us.'

'You charged her rent for sleeping on this?'

Nodded.

'I think she needs help.'

'Needs a good slappin', if you ask me.'

She looked like the Chrissie who'd turned up at the pool.

'Can't you give her a second chance?'

Chrissie looked away. The second chance was long gone.

'Where is she?'

'How the hell should I know?'

'Did you give her anything?'

'Aye, a rucksack and a sleeping bag. I gave her plenty.'

'But she gets panic attacks. You've gotta help her.'

'What's this, a charity appeal on behalf of Spider?' Chrissie squeezed her hands together. 'So how much money did she give you?'

Don't think Chrissie would have let me in if she knew how much I had.

'Fifty p.'

'Fifty bloody p,' she shouted. 'You've gorra be taking the piss.'

'It's all she could afford,' I said, digging the coin out of my pocket and holding it out.

Chrissie slapped my hand away. The coin flew somewhere.

'Listen here, kidda. I suggest you get your arse oot of here before me boyfriend gets back. Fifty effing p.'

I managed to scoop my bum cheeks out of the sofa and Chrissie pushed me into the hall.

'Just want to know she's okay.'

'Get the eff out of here, will you?' she screamed.
Chrissie opened the front door and shoved me out.
The door slammed shut.

Sixteen

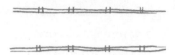

I stood on the street, breathing hard.

Couldn't believe what had happened. What I'd heard. Spider was out there, somewhere, on the streets. I tried to imagine what that would be like, living outdoors, without a bed, a mattress, a laptop, a TV, a toilet. You get all those when you're in a family. Like free gifts.

How would I cope if I was Spider? Probably badly. I swim in Ilkley Lido, so I'm not soft. But I like the heating on when it's cold. And a fan when it's hot. And I don't enjoy wooden chairs for long. And I love a long, hot shower. To survive the streets you must have to be hard as nails. Spider's had practice at it. But that's not to say she's got used to it. I saw the terror on her face when she talked to me about it. Not sure it's something you could ever get used to.

'We can't ignore her, can we, Dex?'

He looked at me with extra-sad eyes. Clearly agreed with me.

I've got nowhere. I've got no one.

'Let's have a look around Ilkley, in case she's still here.'

I took Dexter high on to the moor. Unlikely Spider would come here. Too windswept. Too cold. But you never know. Said she wanted to go up to the rocks one day. Maybe that's where she'd gone. Not many people on the moor. If Spider wanted to escape it would be the perfect spot. The bracken on the lower slopes was as thick as a jungle. You could disappear in there and never be found. But in a strange way I realised the people on the streets were already invisible. Nobody paying them any attention as they go about their lives. How many homeless people had I walked past without thinking about it? Hundreds? Thousands? And how many more had been like Spider? Hidden from view. In a home, but without a home.

I sent Dexter into the foliage for a look and threw in the occasional, 'Spider.' But the name disappeared on the wind.

We walked higher up the moors, past the old spa cottage, and on to Ilkley Crags. It was even colder here. And I knew what Spider thought about the cold. We kept on going until we reached the Twelve Apostles. Not the actual Apostles. Stone ones. At school they told us this was a Bronze-Age circle. An old-fashioned clock, probably. One that it was impossible to tell the time with.

But the bracken here was short, scrubby. Trimmed by all that wind. Be hard to find a place you couldn't be spotted. Dexter and I kept on looking anyway. Further on we found the Pancake Stone, a big, flat rock nestling on top of another one. Just the sort of place you could shelter under. Had a peek, but apart from an empty cheese-and-onion crisp packet, found nothing.

We came down off the moors.

The following day we headed up the Dales Way, the path that leads to Lake Windermere, over one hundred kilometres away. Not sure Spider would go that far, but I decided to walk down the valley and see what I could find. Unfortunately, at this time of year there were loads of walkers about. People with ski poles, but no skis. Middle-aged men and women in floppy hats, shorts and heavy-looking boots. Dexter and I had a good rummage in the bushes and trees along the banks of the River Wharfe, but we drew a blank.

While I knew the town, I didn't know every nook and cranny. Only lived here a short while, and most of that time had been spent in school. I couldn't really ask Tourist Information, *Where are the best places to hide in Ilkley?* They'd think I'd done something wrong and call the police.

Decided to spend one more day looking for Spider.

Thought she might have hidden herself somewhere quiet, like in the woods. The nearest was Middleton

Woods, behind the lido. With the sun unable to break out from its prison of thick clouds, I walked Dexter down Middleton Avenue, past the huge houses on Curly Hill and up towards the trees. We reached the V-shaped gap in the fence and climbed through.

The place was popular with people who wanted some shade or didn't fancy the steep paths up to Ilkley Moor. Little tracks criss-crossed the woods. If Spider was here, I reckon she'd bury herself away in the foliage, far from the dog walkers and the joggers. We crossed a bridge made of logs, left the track and went into the knee-high ferns that spread out in every direction.

'Dex, find Spider. The person, not the creature.'

He looked at me as if I was an idiot. Wished I could have hired a bloodhound for the day.

We went further into the shade.

'Spider,' I called.

Nothing.

'Come on, Dex. Let's go get some food.'

As we were heading out, I glimpsed a blue shape further down the slope. It wasn't a colour you saw here, apart from bluebells, but they'd all been and gone. We moved towards it through the ferns. As I got nearer I could see that it was a piece of plastic, resting on a tepee made of sticks, the type of crude den that kids make. Then I saw another shape at the bottom. It was a long, black oblong. A sleeping bag.

I hurried towards it.

'Spider.'

As I got close a white face appeared from the black. It had dabs of dirt on it. The hair was lank. The lips were cracked and dry. Two screwed-up eyes turned my way.

'Tyler, is that you?'

Seventeen

Spider hadn't been lying to me. She really did have nowhere to go. Apart from a wood. She unzipped her sleeping bag and crawled out as if she was an old woman. Spider was wearing the same jeans and top she always wore. Also had her trainers on. Guess she had nowhere else to put them, apart from her feet. She didn't seem too happy that I'd found her. As if she was ashamed.

'What yous deein here?'

'Looking for you.'

'Why?'

''Cos I wanted to.'

Dexter went up and licked Spider's hand. She ruffled his fur.

'How d'ya find me?'

'A sniffer dog,' I said, giving Dexter credit he didn't deserve.

She unzipped a compartment in her rucksack, pulled her glasses out and put them on. It made her look like the old Spider again. She sat down awkwardly on the ground, like her bones were aching. I sat next to her.

'What happened with Chrissie?'

She took in two full nostrils worth of air. 'When I got back she was there. So was he. Me rucksack packed. Sleeping bag. Nowt more to say.'

'Did you ask them if they'd change their mind?'

Spider laughed. 'No, Tyler, I didn't get me begging mat out. If you'd seen their faces, you'd know. That was it. End of story. I'm leavin'.'

I knew what Chrissie could be like. Imagine it was twice as bad with her boyfriend there.

Spider played with a leaf.

'What you gonna do? Can't stay here for ever.'

A big exhale told me she knew that.

I guess someone would eventually find her and call the police or a farmer, or whoever owns this place. They'd tell the council or the person who looks after things like this. They'd find her a flat. Or maybe another sofa. Wasn't sure how these things worked. Or didn't work. But something would happen. Eventually.

Spider looked as though she was beyond caring.

But I was wrong.

'I-I had a plan,' she said. 'Not the best one ever, but a plan.'

'What was it?'

'To stay here. Make some money. Get me own flat.'

Spider couldn't scrabble enough together to pay for her swimming lessons. Would take years to get enough for a flat.

'Why not get another job?'

Spider played with the leaf. 'For full-time work you need a permanent address: *the woods, thirtieth tree from the left.*'

'What about your cleaning job?'

'Chrissie got me that. And she doesn't want me back. Imagine me, knocking on someone's door looking like this, asking if they want their house cleaned.'

A door-slam in the face.

I wondered if I should tell her I'd been to see Chrissie. Couldn't make things any worse.

'I went to see your cousin.'

If Spider was surprised she hid it well. 'What she say?'

'Said she couldn't do anything. It wasn't her flat.'

Spider crumpled the leaf and threw it away. 'Her bastard boyfriend had it in for me. Soon as I saw him, knew me days were numbered. He hated me. Wouldn't bother him if I was dead.'

Now I knew why Spider didn't talk much about herself or her life. Who'd want to hear this story? Depressing as hell, like one of those dramas Mum watches.

'Is there anything I can do to help?'

'Aye, clear off.'

Shocked. But I saw she wasn't really cross.

'You've got your own life, man, don't get messed up in mine.'

'I meant like getting you a bottle of water or something. A Mars bar, maybe.'

Spider smiled. 'That's dead kind. But you've done enough. You taught me to swim. Never thought that would happen. Not in a million years.'

'Swimming's not much use round here?'

'Too bloody right,' she said, looking at the foliage that seemed to envelop us. 'As much use as a flat tyre.'

Spider would have said something funnier, but I guess it's hard to be funny when nothing's funny any more.

'Okay, you can get me a few things.'

I got my phone out ready to make a list.

'Books would be good.'

'Books?'

'Aye.'

Didn't have Spider down as a reader, but I guess they'd help her pass the time, one thing she had loads of. I wrote 'books' with my finger.

'Some food, and water, and toilet paper.'

'Is that it?'

She paused.

'And tampons.'

'Tampons?

'Tampons.'

Eighteen

•
•
•

Luckily Mum had taken Tallulah to see Gran and Grandad in Derby, so I had the run of the house. But needed to be careful not to take too much stuff or she'd think we'd been burgled. I made a couple of chicken-salad sandwiches, grabbed some apples and bananas, then took a couple of water bottles from the fridge. I raided the downstairs loo for a few toilet rolls. Mum's always got stacks of them, as if dysentery is about to hit our house.

Then I went into the sitting room to find some books. I'd forgotten to ask Spider what genre she preferred. Was she a crime lover? Maybe she'd seen enough of that already. Romance? Didn't strike me as the soppy type. Biographies? Not a clue who she liked or hated. Dystopian novels? She'd probably had enough weirdness in her life not to want to read about that. I grabbed four books randomly. Hoped there'd be something she liked.

Then the tricky bit. Tampons.

I could have bought some from Boots but that would have been too embarrassing. Decided to see if Mum had some. Went upstairs to the bathroom. I felt bad. But not bad enough to stop me. I opened a cabinet, and underneath a mountain of moisturisers, found what I was looking for. I looked inside the box. It was half-full. I had no idea how many to take. Should have googled periods. I guessed Mum wouldn't miss three. So that's how many I took.

I thought of waiting until later to take the bag to Spider, but then I imagined Mum coming back.

Tyler, why are you leaving our house with a sandwich, toilet rolls, a bag of books and three of my tampons?

Get out of that one.

I decided to leave right away. Weighed down with two heavy bags, I hurried through town and across the bridge towards the woods. All the way there I kept my eyes peeled for Michele. She'd want to know where I was going, and what was in the bag, and why I looked so guilty. There are some situations no amount of lying can get you out of.

I climbed through the V and stumbled through the undergrowth to the makeshift tepee. But the sleeping bag was flat, her rucksack buried in the foliage.

'Spider,' I shouted.

No sign of her.

She could have gone to the toilets down by the river or the supermarket to grab some free samples. Considered waiting for her to come back, but I didn't fancy sitting in a wood, with nothing to do, so I took the bags, shoved them inside her sleeping bag, and zipped it up.

'Spider,' I yelled again.

To no avail.

I turned and headed home.

That evening I started my second job of the summer. The Drivers were a family in the street next to ours who Mum had met through Tallulah. They had a daughter the same age. Having gone on holiday to Turkey they'd left a key for my mum and a set of instructions.

> *Feed cats twice a day – cat food in pantry*
> *Top up cat water bowls*
> *Water plants when dry*
> *Double lock door when you leave*
> *Put alarm on*
> *Thanxxxx*
> *Chloe Driver*

'Got all that?' said Mum, handing me the key, the alarm code and the note.

'Not exactly complicated, is it?'

'Do you know when a plant needs water?'

'When it looks dead?'

'No, Tyler, when the leaves are drooping. You can also do the finger test. If you push your finger up to the first knuckle it's moist. If you can't get your finger in, it's too dry.'

Couldn't stop a snigger.

'Please try to act your age.'

I headed round to the Drivers' and let myself in. They were mad on foliage. Every single room had been infiltrated by plants in pots. On bookshelves, in corners, on bedside tables, on the piano, on the toilets. It was more like a greenhouse than a house-house. Why not just have one big plant, like a tree? People have some funny hobbies.

I decided not to do the finger test. I'd water them whether they needed it or not. Plants can't drown, can they?

And then there were the cats. I read the names on their bowls – Heathrow and Gatwick. They both eyed me suspiciously as I entered the kitchen. *Who the hell are you and what are you doing in our house?*

Dogs never give you looks like that, but mistrust comes naturally to cats. They not only hate you, they know better than you. I wondered if Michele had been a cat in a previous life.

I topped up their water and filled their bowls with tiny brown pellets. The cat who could have been Gatwick squirmed up against my leg. I gave him a gentle stroke and got a vicious scratch for my efforts.

'You little sod.'

Gatwick looked at me, as if to say, *Get over it, wimp.*

I should be getting danger money.

Having fed and watered every living thing I could find, I went home.

'How was that?' asked Mum, as I slammed the front door.

'Best experience of my life.'

I clomped up to my room and lay on the bed. I thought of Spider on her bed made of leaves and twigs. How on earth would she put up with that night after night after night? I'd got bored in the woods after about ten seconds. How would she read when it got dark? What would she do if someone stumbled across her? And how could she stay dry when the weather turned? Thin sticks and that plastic sheet weren't going to stop much.

I've got no one. I've got nowhere.

But what could I do? My only talent was to go up and down pools at an above-average speed. I couldn't keep taking her food and toiletries every day. Mum would find out eventually. And soon I'd be back at school, with homework and sport. When would I find time to visit her?

That night we had another family dinner. Mum clearly believed in the power of food.

'This is nice,' she said.

Wasn't sure whether she meant her pasta or the Jacksons sitting round a table together, armed with knives and forks, not stabbing each other.

I decided to raise the Spider issue. But removed the word Spider.

'I found someone today.'

My parents both stopped, mid-chew, like startled cattle.

'Found someone?' said Dad.

'Yeah, a woman in the woods.'

'Oh my god, was she dead?' exclaimed Mum, clasping a hand to her mouth. She'd clearly watched too much horrible stuff online.

'No, she was breathing. She was in a sleeping bag.'

'Maybe she's on a camp-out,' said Tallulah, sucking up a length of spaghetti, leaving a Bolognese trail up her chin.

'No, she was on her own.'

'You spoke to her?' said Mum.

'Yeah, found her in Middleton Woods.'

'What were you doing all the way down there?'

'Taking Dex for a walk.'

'How old is she?' said Mum, eyeing me suspiciously.

'I didn't check her passport. Twenty-five, maybe.'

Didn't want to say eighteen. The same age as the girl I'd given lessons to.

'Didn't think you got homeless people in Ilkley,' said Dad, taking a big mouthful of wine.

'Guess anyone can fall on hard times,' said Mum.

'I reckon most of it's self-inflicted.'

'That's a huge generalisation, Clive.'

'Not saying they're all like that, but I bet lots of them are. Drink, drugs.'

'She's not like that,' I said, more loudly than I'd intended.

Mum and Dad stopped eating to stare at me.

'How do you know she's not like that?' asked Mum.

'I spoke to her. Drink and drugs have got nothing to do with it. She's got nowhere to live, that's all. She needs help.'

'If she needs help, it's a job for the experts,' said Mum, sipping her wine. 'Like you and your swimming lessons.'

'You could build her a tree den,' said Tallulah, failing to grasp the seriousness of the situation.

'There must be something we can do,' I said.

'Has she got food and water?' said Mum.

Yes, ours.

Nodded.

'Cans of cider?'

'Clive!'

Mum was more sympathetic than Dad. I guess her job is to stop people getting hurt. But, even so, neither of them seemed to have grasped the mess Spider was in. I suppose when you've got everything it's hard to imagine having nothing.

Silence.

'I'll call someone in the morning,' said Mum.

'Why not call them now?'

'Because it's late. I'll call them tomorrow.'

Nineteen

The combination of a comfy bed and no school was irresistible. I got up at half-past ten and padded downstairs.

'Have you called yet?'

Mum turned, a startled look on her face. 'Shoot, forgot all about that.'

'Thought your job's all about caring for people.'

'Of course I care, Tyler, but believe you me, there are worse things in the world than being homeless.'

'Tell that to a homeless person.'

This time it was Mum who sighed.

'Tell me what you know.'

'She's from up north. Her mum died. She hates her dad. Got a cousin in Ilkley who doesn't want her in her house any more. She had a job as a cleaner, but lost it. And she's got tattoos down her arms, sorry, arm.'

Mum stared at me intently. 'Must have been a long conversation.'

'She's a bit of a motor-mouth.'

'Okay, I'll call someone. She's in Middleton Woods?'

Nodded.

'Let's hear what they've got to say.'

Mum hurried into the study to find the number, while I sat on the sofa, feeling pleased with myself. At last things were happening.

I heard Mum on the phone but couldn't tell how it was going. Mum's got one of those voices that doesn't really go places. The call didn't last very long. Guess it was quite an easy case for them. *Young woman in sleeping bag in woods needs room. Right, we'll send a van up and get her.*

The door to the study opened. I could tell from Mum's face that it hadn't quite gone the way I wanted. Or Spider, for that matter. She sat down next to me.

'I spoke to someone at StreetLink. I told them where she was, and what had happened. They said they'd pass the information on to the local authority.'

'So they'll find her a place?'

'I don't know, Tyler. They said they'll look into it. I gave them my details. They said they'd let me know how everything's gone.' She glanced at her watch. 'I need to crack on.'

Mum went back into her office and closed the door.

It seemed that Spider's luck was finally turning.

That afternoon Mum took Tallulah to a tennis camp.

I took the opportunity to fill a carrier bag with bananas, apples, energy bars and bottled water, and headed back to Middleton Woods.

'You're a bloody star, you are,' said Spider, peeling a banana and eating it faster than you're meant to. She glugged from a bottle of water and wiped her lips. 'And books as well.'

'Were they okay?'

'Apart from the biography of Oliver Cromwell. Still, it'll come in handy if I run out of toilet paper.'

'Got some good news.'

Spider looked intrigued.

'Mum rang someone called StreetLink. Gave them your details. Someone's gonna come for you. They'll find you a room in a hostel.'

Spider spat out her banana and glared at me. 'Did I ask you to do that? Did I?'

'No, but…'

'I'm not gannin with them.'

'But they'll help you.'

'Didn't help last time.'

'What do you mean?'

Spider's skinny chest grew bigger as she took in air.

'After I'd run out of sofas up north, got put in a hostel. There was a guy there…' she said, her voice fading to almost nothing.

Spider stayed silent, but her face told me the story.

Something terrible had happened. She kicked at a shrub as the memory caused havoc inside her head.

'Did you ask to be moved?'

Spider shook her head. 'Too late for that. Had to get away.'

'Why didn't you tell someone?'

''Cos they wouldn't believe me.'

'Didn't you trust them?'

'No, I didn't trust them. Trust is when crap happens. I trusted me dad. I trusted Chrissie. I trusted you.'

'Me?'

'Yes, you. All I asked for was some food and stuff. I didn't want a hostel.' She bent forward, her face disappearing into her grubby hands. 'Just want me own room, in me own place. That's all I was trying to get here.'

'Maybe the hostels round here are different.'

'And maybe they're not.'

Silence again.

'You can't have bad luck for ever.'

'What the hell do you know about bad luck? What bad things have ever happened to you? You moan about moving from London to this beautiful place. You moan because you haven't had a summer holiday. You moan when I don't give you the exact money. You've absolutely no idea how bloody awful life can get, no bloody idea at all.'

Didn't like being talked to like this. I knew she'd had a crap life. Was having a crap life. But I didn't deserve this.

I jumped to my feet.

'I'm going home.'

'Alreet for some,' came the Geordie voice as I stomped through the trees.

I was fist-clenchingly angry. I'd given her swimming lessons. I'd tracked her down. I'd brought her food, books, tampons. I'd even got Mum to ring a charity to help her. And this was the thanks I got.

Stuff her.

I walked quickly home, head down, breathing hard.

I was halfway up the Grove when a voice stopped me dead.

'Tyler.'

Michele was standing right in front of me, looking fit, as ever.

'Are you ghosting me?' she said, staring to me.

''Course not.'

'I've been texting you.'

'I texted you back.'

'Twice. I texted six times.'

'Didn't realise it was a competition.'

Michele looked annoyed.

'I'm sorry. I've been busy.'

Michele laughed. 'You, busy?'

'Yeah, the neighbours' cats need feeding.'

'What are you making them – Sunday lunch?'

I let loose a nervous laugh.

'Where've you been?'

'For a walk.'

'Could have asked me.'

'I'm sorry,' I said, even though I wasn't. I just wanted this conversation to end. Especially after what had happened in the woods. 'Why don't we meet at the café? Twelve o'clock tomorrow.'

'Is that what you really want?'

'Yeah, of course.'

'Don't sound so enthusiastic.'

'I am.'

There was another reason to meet up with Michele. To get the latest on Luke.

'I just want things to work out,' said Michele.

'Yeah,' I said, despite having no idea precisely what she meant.

I turned to leave.

'You've got mud all over your shoes. Where have you been, Tyler?'

Twenty

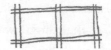

'**You are so** lucky you're a dog, Dex.'

He wagged his tail in agreement.

'Spider and Michele. Why don't they teach you about stuff like this in school?'

We strolled slowly around Ilkley Tarn.

'Spider wants a home. Michele wants a boyfriend. I can give one of them what they want, but not the other. Two girls, from different worlds.'

I threw a stone in the water.

'Michele is spoiled. Spider is the opposite of spoiled. So why did she turn down the chance to get a room in a hostel? Why did she shout at me like that?'

Dexter had no idea.

'Maybe what Spider said was right, Dex. How on earth could I, living in Fairspew, give advice to someone like her?'

I looked across the tarn. Summer seemed to have gone into hiding. Dark clouds scudded over the hilltops, trees were behaving erratically in the wind. I took out my phone and googled the weather. The next forty-eight hours were filled with little blue dots. Rain. Across the valley lay Spider, her only protection a small plastic sheet on top of a triangle of twigs.

'Wonder how fast the charity will send someone to find her. Might be on their holidays. Could take days. Weeks. And even if they come, what chance is there she'll go with them?'

Faced with such a tricky question Dex decided to chase a duck.

'Come on. Let's go home.'

An hour later the rain came, beating its rhythm against my bedroom window. Not the gentle stuff that leaves your face lightly spritzed, the heavy stuff that makes you feel like you've been punched. Hard. I thought of Spider rearranging the plastic sheet over her head, trying and failing to keep the wet off, crawling into her sleeping bag, the rain soaking the material, soaking her, once again immersed in cold water, but this time with no dry towel waiting for her.

She'd made me angry. But the anger had been diluted. I needed to help her. But what could I do? I lay there, staring at the ceiling, thinking.

About once a year I have an idea that a teacher would mark as good. I grinned. I'd just had one that could be marked as brilliant. I jumped off my bed, went downstairs and grabbed a waterproof jacket from a peg by the kitchen door.

'Where you going now?' said Mum, who was peeling potatoes at the sink.

'Out.'

'It's pouring.'

'I'm a swimmer. I like water.'

Not a bad answer.

Before she could say more, I dashed outside and headed through town towards the woods. The clouds had become guns, lowering themselves into position, firing round after round in my direction. It was like being in a water fight. One I was never going to win.

Hunched forward, I strode up the road into Middleton Woods. The trees provided some protection from the downpour, but not enough, the rain finding a way through, the way it does. My jeans were sodden by the time I got to Spider's den. I bent down and there she was, huddled under the sheet, her wet face poking out from beneath the plastic.

'You again,' she said, staring at me through rain-spattered glasses.

I pulled the plastic sheet off her.

'What the hell d'ya think ya deein?'

'We're leaving.'

'Where to?'

'Follow me.'

Spider would normally dig her trainers in and refuse to budge, but I think she'd had enough of the woods, and the rain, and the cold. With much cursing she folded up her wet sleeping bag, attached it to the top of her rucksack, and flung it over her back.

'Where are we going?'

'You'll find out soon enough.'

Spider and I made our way out of the woods, past the lido and up Denton Road. Luckily the wind and rain had blown everyone indoors, but it didn't stop fear building up inside me. Because what I was about to do wasn't entirely legal.

Twenty-one

Spider dumped her rucksack on the kitchen floor and sat down heavily on a chair. She took her glasses off and wiped them on a frilly tablecloth.

'Where the bloody hell are we?'

'Keep your voice down,' I whispered. 'We're in the house of Mr and Mrs Driver.'

'Who the crappin' heck are they?'

'The couple who want me to water their plants while they're on holiday.'

The penny dropped. Spider put her glasses back on and grinned.

'They won't be back for another five days. You've got a roof, a loo, running water, a shower.'

'A bed?'

'Sorry, you're gonna have to crash on the sofa.'

'Sofas and me are like that,' she said, twisting her long fingers round each other, as if they were in love.

'But you've gotta be careful,' I said, pacing the

kitchen. 'I'm the only one who's meant to be here. You mustn't look out of the window or open the front door or go in the garden, wandering round.' I racked my brain for other things to watch out for. 'And don't go raiding their fridge. Dinner's not included. And if you have a shower, make sure everything's put back exactly the way you found it. No wet towels on the floor.'

Spider looked bored at my ever-growing list of instructions.

'And don't watch TV or listen to the radio. You need to keep the noise down.'

The Drivers lived in a terraced house and while the walls looked thick enough to stop rockets, sounds could worm their way through.

'So I can't even gan for a walk?'

'Yes, but keep your walking indoors. Where you can't be seen.'

'Not gonna get much exercise walking roond a toilet,' said Spider, running her fingers through her wet hair. 'Like being a prisoner.'

'But it's a dry prison.'

I went to a kitchen cupboard, took out two glasses, filled them with water and gave one to Spider. I looked outside, my nerves still jangling, thinking someone might have spotted us. Spider drained the glass in a couple of seconds, wiped her mouth, and put the glass down on the table.

'Sorry for shoutin' at yous in the woods. You're the only one roond here who's done owt for me. Mam always said "divvent bite the hand that feeds you". I chewed your whole bloody arm off.' She fiddled with a hole in her jeans. 'I was so tired, and so cold, so bloody cold.'

'It's okay.'

Spider looked at me. 'What you deein all this for, putting yersel at risk?'

Good question.

I could have walked away from Spider, the way people do, thinking she must be responsible for the mess she's in. But I knew Spider's situation wasn't her fault. Even her own cousin wouldn't lift a finger. Her life had shattered into a million pieces, and there was no one to help her put it back together. Maybe there was another reason I was doing this. Over the last few weeks I'd got to know her. And while I didn't fancy her, not in a Michele sort of way, I admired her spirit. I liked her. And if you like people, aren't you meant to do things for them?

'Need to go. Mum and Dad'll be wondering where I've gone.'

Spider nodded.

'I'll come back and see you tomorrow.'

I turned to walk towards the door.

'Tyler.'

Stopped.

Spider got up from her chair, came over and gave me the longest, wettest hug I'd ever had. I felt her stale breath on my cheek. I smelled the sweat that had leaked into her clothes. I felt her long, damp hair brushing my face. But although I didn't like it, not a bit, I let her hold me. She needed to know that there was still someone in her world who cared about her. I'd let it go on as long as she wanted.

Spider finally released me from her grasp. When I stepped back, I saw her eyes were filled to the brim with tears. She took off her glasses to wipe them away.

'Now look what you've made me do,' she sniffed. 'Gan on, get yersel oot of here.'

Good to know there's one person on planet earth I can make happy. I put my coat on, opened the front door and hurried home through the monsoon. Dad was in the kitchen, drying a plate.

'Where the heck have you been?' he shouted. 'You missed supper.'

'At the Drivers'. Doing my chores.'

'You're absolutely soaked. Their house isn't that far.'

'Tell the rain that.'

'Your plate's in the oven,' he grunted, going back to his drying.

I hung up my dripping coat, went to the kitchen to retrieve my meal, doubts still nibbling away at me. Had I remembered everything back at the Drivers'?

No.

I put the plate down, dashed to the utility room and grabbed my coat from a peg.

'Where you off to now?' shouted Dad.

'Not sure I left enough food for the cats.'

I ran all the way to the Drivers' house. I was right to be worried. The house was lit up like Oxford Street at Christmas. I opened the front door and ran inside.

'Spider,' I called, as loudly as I dared.

'In here, man,' came a voice from the kitchen.

I dashed in to find her sitting on a chair, in the middle of a staring competition with Heathrow. Or it could have been Gatwick.

'Bloody awful, these two. More like panthers. One's already taken a swipe.'

'Never mind the cats, you've turned half the lights on. You might as well hang up a neon sign, *Burglars at Work.*'

'Was dead dark in those woods at night. Nice to have a few bulbs on.'

I hurried around the house, turned off all the lights and came back to the kitchen.

'Mess things up, divvent I?'

'No, Spider, you divvent mess things up, but you've gorra be careful.'

'That's the worst Geordie accent I've ever heard.'

I gave her a half-hearted smile and went home to

a lukewarm dinner for one. Was glad no one else was there. They'd be asking questions. The way they usually did. Could do with a bit of quiet time. It didn't last long. Mum came and sat next to me.

'Why did you dash off tonight, Tyler?'

'Finishing my chores.'

She looked like she didn't believe a word.

But before she could dig any deeper her phone pinged. Mum can never wait to see who's messaging her. Retrieving the phone from her pocket, she read the text, and turned to me.

'You did say that woman was in Middleton Woods?'

'Yeah,' I replied, my heart beginning to race. 'Why?'

'Got a text from the council. They sent someone to search for her and found nothing.' Mum put her phone down and looked at me. 'You don't know where she could have gone, do you?'

Twenty-two

'Spider,' I whispered. 'Spider, it's Tyler.'

Gatwick and Heathrow appeared from the kitchen to see who it was, and if they were worth attacking.

'Spider.'

No reply.

I opened the sitting-room door and saw a long shape, underneath a blanket, one tattooed arm wrapped around a cushion. Even though the place was bathed in sunlight, Spider was fast asleep, snoring gently. Reckoned she must have a week's worth of sleep to catch up on. I decided to leave her while I did my chores.

Gatwick and Heathrow squirmed around my legs. I figured the only time cats love you is feeding time. On all other occasions you serve no purpose whatsoever. I filled their bowls with tiny pellets and topped up their water. Today's visit included a new job, retrieving the body of a dead mouse from next to the fridge. Cats like to bring you deceased animals. Some kind of peace offering for the scratches they give you. Why don't they ever bring in anything useful like a packet of crisps, or money?

Then it was time for the indoor rainforest. I didn't bother with Mum's finger test. I watered them until nothing more would go in. When I'm older I won't waste water on plants. It's all going in one place – a heated indoor swimming pool. Plants won't be allowed in my house.

Having finished my jobs, I had a look around to see that everything was in order. Needless to say, it wasn't.

'Spider,' I said, shaking her awake.

'Worrisit?' she groaned, turning two scrunched eyes on me. 'Are the people back?'

'No, but there's a soaking wet towel on the bathroom floor, soap splattered in the shower, plates and cups in the sink.'

'I'll sort it before they get back, man,' she said, lifting herself up on her elbow.

'Be a lot better if you did it as you went along.'

'I'll try.'

'But what about…'

Ring. Ring.

The front doorbell.

Spider and I shared shocked faces.

'Who is it?' whispered Spider.

'How should I know? You'd better hide.'

'Might be the postman.'

'Don't care. Just hide.'

Spider got up from the sofa as quickly as freshly woken limbs will allow, hurried into a study off the sitting room and closed the door.

Ring. Ring.

Clearly whoever it was didn't know that the Drivers were on holiday. Probably a parcel from Amazon. Mum gets millions of those.

I walked down the hall.

Ring. Ring.

'Okay, okay.'

Opened the door.

Michele.

Twenty-three

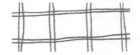

'Hi, Tyler.'

'Er, hi, Michele.'

Despite a downturn in the weather, Michele was dressed for a heatwave, in a flimsy blue summer dress and sandals.

'Don't look very pleased to see me.'

That gets a *Guinness World Records* certificate for understatement.

'No, I'm very pleased,' I said. 'Very, very pleased.'

'Now you're laying it on way too thick.'

'Who told you I was here?'

'Your mum. I went to your house to find you.'

Why today, of all days?

'Can I come in?'

'I'm just leaving. Finished my jobs,' I said, moving forward.

'But isn't that your coat on the hall peg?'

Before I could grab it, Michele had burst in, like a police officer on a drugs raid.

'I love seeing other people's houses,' she said, looking around.

I should have thrown her out, but that would have set her alarm bells off. Why wouldn't I let her see inside an empty house? Almost empty house. And then there were the other clues. The cutlery and glasses in the sink. The wet towel in the bathroom. Why would I have a shower in a stranger's house when I had a perfectly good shower at home?

Michele walked slowly down the hall, studying the pictures, the furnishings, as though she was in a museum.

'There's nothing to see,' I said.

'I'll be the judge of that.'

She reached the kitchen.

'Oh, they've got cats,' she exclaimed excitedly.

'Yes, Heathrow and Gatwick.'

'What cute names.'

Michele bent down and stroked the cat who I think is Gatwick. I'm not what you'd call a violent person, but for once I hoped that the cat would do what he does best, causing her to run screaming out of the front door. But, no, instead of getting his claws out, Gatwick rolled on to his back for a tummy tickle.

Cats are so bloody unreliable.

'Aren't they adorable?' she said.

I could think of dozens of adjectives for these cats, adorable was not among them.

'Michele, I think we should leave.'

'What's the matter? You're so jittery.'

'It … it's not my house.'

'But they're on holiday, aren't they? They'll never know,' she said, a mischievous glint in her eye.

Michele stopped massaging Gatwick's tummy and got to her feet. 'I'd like to see their bedrooms.'

'No,' I shouted.

'Ooh, listen to Mr Forceful.'

'Please, Michele. They've placed a big responsibility on me. I don't want to ruin it.'

'Such a goody-two-shoes,' she said, walking back down the hall. Michele was leaving.

I breathed out all the breath I'd been holding. But instead of walking to the front door, she turned left into the sitting room.

'Been sleeping on the job?' she said, looking down at the blanket and pillow where Spider had been lying a couple of minutes ago.

She put her hand on the blanket. 'It's still warm. And I thought you came here to work,' said Michele, eyeing me suspiciously.

'I … I was really tired this morning. Didn't sleep well. The wind. The rain. Lashing the window. You know how it is.'

'And it smells,' she said, sniffing.

'Didn't have a chance for a shower.'

But before she could quiz me further about my sleeping habits, her attention was drawn to something else – a mud-covered rucksack by the coffee table.

'I ... I ... think it's Mr Driver's.'

'How come he leaves a filthy rucksack in his sitting room?'

Why did I let Michele in?

'Must have forgotten to put it away.'

I prayed to any god who'd have me that Michele wouldn't start looking inside it. Bras, knickers, hair-ties, tampons.

Is Mr Driver having transgender treatment?

There are some holes too deep to climb out of.

Michele turned her attention from the rucksack to me. 'Sit down, Tyler.'

Dutifully, I sat next to her. I finally realised what she had in mind. The empty house, her, me. What better opportunity to get to know someone better?

Michele put a warm hand on my thigh. 'I've been thinking a lot about you, Tyler.'

Is it possible to have a wonderful dream and a nightmare both at the same time? Because that's what was happening. I'd conjured up all sorts of unforgettable scenarios with Michele, but these scenarios didn't take place in the house of a couple I was doing jobs for, with the homeless girl I was helping in a room next door.

Michele shuffled towards me, until our legs were as close as chicken thighs in a packet.

'Sorry I got a bit spiky in the café, but I thought there was something going on between you and that skinny cow from the pool.'

'She's not that thin.'

'And those glasses make her look like a frog.'

'I think they suit her.'

I prayed that Spider couldn't hear any of this. I imagined her bursting through the door armed with a letter opener, writing 'bastard' on Michele's forehead.

'Let's not talk about her. She's gone.'

'Good riddance.'

Michele moved her face to me. Close. I turned away to look at a watercolour of a Highland stag.

'What's the matter?'

Where could I begin? Apart from us not being as alone as she'd wanted, there was another major issue – Michele herself. While I fancied her as much as I'd ever fancied anyone, I was confused too. There was the breath-defying run, her jealousy, her horrible remarks about Spider, and last but by no means least, Luke – her ex-boyfriend, who was going to kill me. None of this was conducive to horniness.

I bet half the boys in class, no make that ninety-five per cent, would like to find themselves in my shoes, almost alone in a house with Michele Hastings. But I felt scared, miles out of my depth, the shore a faint line on the horizon.

I stole a line I'd heard in one of Mum's TV dramas. 'I don't think I'm ready for this right now.'

'When will you be ready?' said Michele, looking at her watch.

'Not sure.'

'Don't be so silly.'

Michele put her hand round the back of my head and pulled our faces together. Our lips collided in the most stupendous fashion. This moment could have been one of my most enjoyable ever, but for two people, one four metres away, the other still on holiday, planning my murder.

We finally came up for air.

'Wasn't so bad, was it?' said Michele. She was the Queen of Wicked Grins.

'Not bad at all,' I said, smiling nervously.

I'd be lying if I said I hadn't enjoyed that. I only wish we were doing it somewhere else.

'We could do other things,' said Michele, scrabbling her fingers up my thigh to the region only my hand went. 'Would you like me to close the curtains?'

While that would solve one problem, what Michele really needed to do was build an impenetrable soundproof barrier between this room and the study.

'Not now, Michele. Please.'

'Are you sure?'

'Positive.'

Michele got to her feet. 'Okay, let's do it another time,' she said, her voice drizzled with disappointment.

'Yeah.'

'When are you next feeding the cats?'

Twenty-four

I managed to get Michele out of the house without further incident.

'Are you not coming?' she said, seeing that I was still standing in the doorway.

'Got a few more plants to water.'

'When I arrived you were leaving. Don't mess me around.'

I conjured up a crocodile laugh. 'Me?'

'Yes, you, Tyler Jackson.' She gave me a quick kiss on the lips before heading up the path. 'And text me when you're next coming back?'

'Sure.'

Unsure.

I waited until she'd disappeared out of sight before going back in, closing the door and double locking it. Breath once again returned to my lungs. I clumped into the sitting room to find Spider sitting on the sofa, laughing her head off.

'What's so funny?'

'You.'

I peered out of the window to make sure that Michele was well and truly gone, before sitting down next to her.

'That was bad, Spider.'

'Sounded good from where I was.'

She pushed her glasses up her nose. 'Mind you, I could have lamped her after what she said aboot me looking like a frog. She's got acid for spit, that one.'

I held my head in my hands. A few weeks ago life had been dull, but simple. How had it suddenly turned into this?

'Have you ever had a boyfriend?'

Spider looked away at a picture of Mr and Mrs Driver on their wedding day.

'Aye, Liam, a lad from Byker.'

'Did you love him?'

'At first.'

'What happened?'

'Went off with another lass, Daisy Hodges.' She folded her arms. 'Told me by text.'

The male version of Michele. 'But you know what? He broke me heart, but he also taught me a lesson. Never rush into anything. Same with your lass. Tell her what you want and divvent want, who you want to see and not see. It's not for her to call the shots.'

Spider was right. I didn't want to dive right in and have Michele finish with me by text like Luke. For all I knew she was filling in time until someone better came back from holiday.

'She's gonna come here again, isn't she?'

'Probably.'

'What yous gonna do?'

'Don't know.'

I needed to clear my head of all the questions clogging it up. I reminded Spider of the house rules, walked home for my swimming stuff and went to the lido.

I jumped in the deep end. The cold was like a punch that hit everywhere. Maybe this is what going out with Michele would be like, painful at first, but bearable over time, the more you got used to it. I quickly got into my stroke and fifty lengths later I was done. Climbing from the pool, I wrapped myself in a towel that had been gently cooked by the sun, and lay back on the grass. I think Spider's right about the restorative effects of swimming. I felt calmer, more relaxed. But the calm didn't last long. A storm was on its way.

A lad in baggy Bermuda-style shorts, who looked like a Year Eleven, walked over to me.

'Are you Tyler?'

'Yeah.'

'There was someone looking for you earlier. His name's Luke.'

Twenty-five

I walked home as carefully as I've ever walked, nervously scanning each street and alleyway for anyone who looked vaguely dangerous. But Ilkley wasn't London. There weren't many people around, and those that were wandering were elderly with red, cheery faces and shopping trollies. Not exactly gangland.

When I got home I knocked on the study door.

'Mum?'

'One minute.'

A moment later I pushed the door open to find Mum sitting at the desk, her disappointment with the online world all too clear to see.

'Why do you do this if you hate it so much?'

Mum grabbed her inhaler and took a large swig.

'I'm trying to do my bit to help.'

Seems as though she couldn't have picked a tougher job. We had talks in school about the horrible stuff that goes online. But it seemed there were a thousand times more people posting bad stuff than trying to stop it.

'What do you want, Tyler?'

She knew I only ever interrupted her when I was after something.

'Do you know any other people going on holiday, need pets feeding, plants watering?'

Mum stared out of the window at the garages.

'The Jennings have already been, so have the Lawsons, and the Chamberlains. Think that's it.'

The problem was we hadn't been in Ilkley long enough. If this had been London, we'd have a list a mile long of people I could do jobs for.

'You could put flyers through people's doors.'

It could take ages to find jobs that way. Time wasn't on my side. Or Spider's. She was about to be evicted. But just when I thought there was no way out of this maze, help came from an unexpected source. Dad arrived home with a surprisingly cheerful face on. He must have stopped at a golf course on the way back and got a birdie.

'Okay, everyone, family board meeting,' he said.

We gathered at the dining-room table to hear what he had to say.

'I've got some good news.'

'We're going back to London?'

'No, Tyler.'

'We're getting a jacuzzi?'

'No, Tallulah.'

'You got promoted.'

'No, honey.'

Dad's face was disgruntled. The three suggestions were all far better than his actual surprise. Think he wished he hadn't made such a big deal of whatever it was he was going to tell us.

'You know how disappointed you were that we weren't going away this year?'

Three nodding heads.

'And how hard your mum and I have been working.'

Two nodding heads.

'Well, I've sorted something,'

'We *are* going to Disneyland,' squealed Tallulah.

'No, we're going to North Wales.'

If disappointment could be measured, this one would be the size of an elephant.

'Wales?' said Mum, confused.

'Phil, a guy at work, has a cottage there. Says we can have it for mate's rates. We can go there from Thursday to Monday.'

'Well, that's … different,' said Mum, damning with no praise.

'I was hoping for a tad more enthusiasm.'

'It's only Wales,' said Tallulah.

It may only be Wales to my sister, but to me it was a lifeline.

'I think it's a brilliant idea, Dad,' I said, and for the first time that year I gave him a hug.

That night, after a subdued family dinner, I hurried around to the Drivers', where I found Spider sitting on the floor reading one of Mum's romantic novels from the charity shop. She turned a page corner over and looked up.

'Good news, Spider. We're going on holiday.'

'Us two?'

'No, my family. We're off to Wales.'

'Nice for yous.'

'Don't you get it? The house will be empty for four days. You can stay there.'

Spider nodded and slowly put her book down. From her expression she clearly wasn't as excited about the Wales trip as I'd been. I could see the fear and frustration in her eyes, the pain of the past, the cold, the hunger, the uncertainty, all on repeat.

'Sorry. Knaa you're trying your best,' she said, forcing a smile. 'I'll take y'up on your offer, and then I'm out of here. For good.'

'Where you going?'

She paused as though she wasn't sure.

'Leeds. Got another cousin there. Says I can crash on her sofa.'

Baffled.

'If you've got a cousin in Leeds, why didn't you go straight there?'

'Been sending her texts. Just got back to me. Said I can stay once she's back from Spain.'

Seemed like good news. Although you'd never guess it from the look on her face.

Still no home. Still swapping one sofa for another. But at least she had a plan to leave Ilkley. Wish I could find one.

I grabbed a watering can and went around the house doing my chores. Some of the plants looked yellow, others were droopy with the heat. Wondered if I'd watered them too little, or maybe too much. I remembered in biology that plants need carbon dioxide, so I went round breathing on them.

Having done my bit for the environment, I gave the dangerous animals some pellets, made sure Spider was sitting below window level and headed home.

I was thinking of somewhere to get a spare key cut when a big voice drowned the sound of my footsteps.

'Tyler.'

I turned to see an older lad marching towards me.

'I'm Luke.'

Twenty-six

This was not the Luke I was expecting.

He was short, wiry, with the sort of body whose muscles had gone into hiding. But that wasn't to say that he wasn't dangerous. He could be one of these lads who does karate five times a week and can kill you with a single chop.

'I … I'm sorry, didn't mean to go out with Michele. We're not even dating. We just sort of meet up occasionally to talk. About normal things. Nothing more.'

I'd become fluent in gibberish.

'No idea what tha's talking about,' said Luke, in a strong Yorkshire accent. 'Just came to say – watch tha'self.'

Couldn't have been more surprised if Luke had presented me with flowers.

'Watch tha'self?'

'Aye, can be right mardy that one. Unless tha's worked that out already.'

No idea what mardy meant, but it sounded pretty bad.

'We've only been meeting up for a couple of weeks,' I said.

'Couple of weeks too long, I reckon.'

Now that my heart rate had got back down to double figures, I felt confident enough to ask Luke a question.

'Did she really finish with you by text?'

Luke laughed loudly.

'No, I finished with her, before I went on't holiday. Right clingy, she was. Said I was seein' someone when I wasn't. She'll have tha' jumpin' through 'oops if tha's not careful.'

'Why are you telling me this?'

He stood close, and looked around, as if he'd done something he shouldn't. 'I'm doing the decent thing and warning ya. Trust me.'

'Thanks.'

'No bother.'

He patted me on the shoulder and strode off into the sunset.

Had I really just heard what I'd just heard? Luke didn't want to kill me, he wanted to warn me off his ex-girlfriend. Okay, she was jealous, and possessive, and bossy, and said weird things. But maybe that's normal round here. The problem was I had no one to compare her with. Apart from Spider. And she came with a whole wheelbarrow full of issues.

I arranged to meet Michele down Riverside Gardens.

'Hi, Ty,' she said, smiling broadly.

Hate wearing ties. Hate being called Ty. But I didn't want to start off with an argument. On top of that, she looked hot in a tight retro T-shirt, white shorts and sandals.

'Hi, Michele,' I said, making sure I used all her letters.

She gave me a quick kiss on the lips. They were a bit sticky and tasted of strawberries. Never knew lips could taste of that.

'It's lip balm,' she said, reading my expression.

'Oh.'

But I didn't want her think I hadn't enjoyed it.

'Nice.'

'How's Ilkley's number-one cat feeder?'

'Good. Have you seen Luke?'

'No. Have you?'

'No.'

I wanted to ask her why she'd lied about finishing with him, but I'd accidentally lied to her about not seeing him. You've got to get your lies in the right order or you're stuffed.

'Sorry about the other day,' she said. 'Didn't want to get you into trouble with the owners.'

'It's okay.'

She took my hand. 'What do you want, Ty, I mean, really want?'

This was one of those deep questions I absolutely hate.

'I want to see how it goes.'

'What's that mean?'

It doesn't mean anything. It's seven random words that came out of my mouth at a time of stress.

'I want to take it slowly.'

'If it gets any slower it'll stop.'

She wanted commitment. Quick commitment.

'I like you, Michele.'

'Well, that's a start,' she said, letting her fingers play with mine. 'We're off to Greece this weekend.'

'And we're off to Wales.'

She let go of my fingers.

'Thought you weren't going anywhere.'

'Dad got a cheap place for a few days.'

'That's a shame. Wish you were coming to Crete with me,' she said, taking my hand again. 'Be a bit dull, just me and Mum and Dad.'

'Got no brothers and sisters?'

'Not unless Mum and Dad get frisky in Greece.'

Michele smiled, but in a split-second the smile disintegrated. 'Isn't that the pool girl?'

Oh, sweet potatoes.

Up ahead, walking in a dead-straight line towards us was a tall girl in holey jeans, one arm ink-free, one arm not so much.

'Hi, Tyler,' shouted Spider.

What the hell was she doing out of the Drivers' house?

'Oh, hi,' I muttered, as calmly as I could.

Michele stood up, and the two girls eyed each other up and down.

'I'm Spider,' said Spider, offering a hand.

'Thought your name was Lauren,' said Michele, ignoring the hand and looking daggers at me.

'Lauren's her middle name.'

Spider was about to contradict me, but caught my expression, the one that said, *STFU.*

'And I am Michele,' said Michele, her arms folded tight across her chest. 'So, you finally learned the doggie paddle, did you?'

'No, proper swimmin'. Tyler's a great teacher. Maybe he could teach me the crawl?'

Michele's mouth twisted into an unnatural shape. I'd been under strict instructions to end my lessons with Spider, and here she was, trying to kick-start them again.

'I'd have thought crawling would come natural to you, being a spider.'

Spider ignored her and turned to me.

'Oh, gan on, Tyler. You're brilliant, man. You told me you would.'

When did I ever say that?

'I need to go.'

'Michele,' I called. But she was already striding away at a speed not far off a jog.

'See yous later,' shouted Spider.

'What the hell are you playing at?'

'Said you wanted to finish with her. Thought I'd give yous a helping hand.'

'Never said I wanted to finish with her. She's tricky, that's all. I'm just trying to work her out.' Exhaled hard. 'She was starting to be nice, and then you do this.'

'Sorry, was tryin' to help.'

'And what the hell are you doing out? I told you to stay in.'

'I was bored stupid, man. Needed to get oot. Nobody saw me.'

'How do you know that? People are nosy up here. For some it's all they've got to do.'

'Slipped oot the back garden, and over the fence.'

'The way a burglar would.'

'Needed some fresh air.'

'Ilkley's full of fresh air. Just breathe in. Promise me you won't go walkabout again? Promise me?'

Spider took in some of that air she was after, then let it go.

'Aye, I promise.'

I was starting to have serious doubts about letting Spider stay in our house. I imagined her climbing over the garden wall, someone calling the police, me being sent to a young offenders prison for allowing trespassers on our premises.

'I want you to wait until it's dark before going back.'

'Doesn't get dark for ages.'

'Not my fault.'

I stared at Spider.

'I'm taking a huge risk for you.'

'I won't let you down.'

Prayed she was right.

I fished in my pocket and took out a spare key for Fairspew.

Twenty-seven

It was the day the Drivers were due back.

A team of forensic experts wouldn't pay as much attention to their house as I did. I checked the shower and soap for any signs of eighteen-year-old hair. I made sure the dishes were cleaned and put away. I plumped the sofa to remove any Spider impressions. I cleaned the toilets. I put new toilet rolls on the holders. I hoovered the house from top to bottom. I even wiped the tables and surfaces to remove any fingerprints.

'Should get extra for all this,' said Spider, watching as I made sure the paintings were hung straight.

'I want you to do the same when you leave my house. It's got to be spotless, do you hear? Spotless.'

'I hear.'

Hoped she did. Spider had already put all the lights on in a house that was meant to be empty, stood up in front of the sitting-room window, and walked out of the Drivers' in broad daylight. But that wasn't my only problem. I also had to get her out and back to Middleton Woods. Though I reckoned this hurdle shouldn't be too hard to clear. She'd already left once on her own. And if anyone saw me leaving with her I'd say she was helping me clean the place. If they asked why she was carrying a rucksack I'd say it was full of cleaning products, not stolen laptops.

As it turned out, I didn't have to use any of my excuses. I set the alarm and we left the house. It was early in the morning, the streets in this part of Ilkley were devoid of people. Either still on holiday or at a Neighbourhood Watch meeting. Twenty minutes later we were back at Spider's old home. The sticks and the plastic sheet were still there, and together we arranged them, tepee-style, to create a den.

'I've checked the forecast. It's going to be dry tonight.'

Spider nodded.

'Also got you this,' I said, handing her a piece of paper with the address of our house, and the alarm code, in case she forgot it.

She came over and gave me one of her squeezy hugs.

'Then after staying at our place you can head off to Leeds with your cousin. Get a job. Bloater, isn't that what you say?'

'It's belter,' she muttered.

Thought Spider would be happy the way things were working out, but her face told me otherwise.

'What's up?'

'Knackered.'

Knew it was more than that, but I didn't have time to find out what.

'We leave for Wales tomorrow morning. Wait till it gets dark before going to our house. And whatever you do, don't turn the lights on. Keep away from the windows. Stay quiet. Don't eat too much food. If there are any empty packets or banana skins, take them with you. We're back on Monday. Probably late. Leave early on Monday morning. Very early. Go over the garden wall and up the alleyway. And please, please, please, don't leave a mess. Got that?'

Spider nodded.

'I'll take your number, and text you to make sure everything's okay. You have got a phone?'

''Course I've got a phone.'

Spider went into her rucksack and dug out a battered old mobile with a cracked screen. Wondered how she'd got it. If it was borrowed, or maybe nicked.

We swapped numbers.

'I'll come here and find you when I'm back.'

The fragility of my plan was scaring the life out of me. I was letting a homeless Geordie girl, who I'd only known a few weeks, and who had already ignored my advice, stay in my parents' house.

'Please don't let me down, Spider.'

'Won't.' Spider sat down and patted the earth next to her. 'Sit doon.'

Did.

'Why you deein all these things for me?'

I thought for a bit before replying. The opposite of what I do in school. Yes, what was I doing all this for? Putting myself at risk for someone I hardly knew. The answer finally came to me.

'Because you don't deserve this.'

Spider was far from perfect, but nobody should have to live like this, surfing from sofa to sofa, sleeping rough, with no money, no friends, no job, no future, never sure where they'll spend the night or find their next meal.

Spider lifted her glasses to wipe her eyes.

'But at least now you've got a plan,' I said, touching her shoulder.

'Aye, I've gorra plan,' she replied, with zero enthusiasm.

I picked up a stick and threw it. Swallowed by a lake of green.

'I've got a question for you. Why did you pick me at the lido?'

Spider looked off, as if the answer was out there, in the trees.

'You remind me of me brother, Ryan. He's a canny swimmer too. I miss him like mad.'

Twenty-eight

I was happy to get away. Even if it was just Wales. But my happiness was diluted by the thought of what I was leaving behind. Spider. Chrissie had called her a thief. Maybe we'd get back to see the house stripped. Or a huge group of squatters partying, a massive pile of rubbish in the front garden. It was too late, though. I'd given her a key and we were off on our little holiday.

'You're very quiet,' said Mum, as we drove past places with unpronounceable names.

'Yeah, thinking about Michele.'

'Must be love,' said Mum, nudging Dad.

No, it mustn't.

Hadn't heard from Michele since the meeting with Spider in the park. I could have called her, but what would I say? *Sorry for bumping into a girl you wrongly assume I'm seeing*? No, for once I had nothing to feel guilty about. All I'd done was teach Spider to swim. If you get dumped for that there really is no justice in the world. Also, if Luke was right about her, maybe it was best to keep Michele at arm's length. Let things settle down a bit.

The drive to North Wales was long and dull, made even duller by my parents' choice of music. Dad likes classical music, Mum likes soft music sung by people who are mostly dead. Tallulah had no such problem with the sounds coming from the speakers. She'd downloaded a Disney film and was chuckling away happily in a brightly coloured world where everything turns out fine.

After a drive I thought would never end we turned up a bumpy track that had all us nutting the ceiling, until we finally reached the cottage. It was a small stone building with a slate roof, surrounded by fields filled with sheep, and a stream gurgling away at the bottom of the valley.

'Isn't this gorgeous?' exclaimed Mum.

If you like that sort of thing.

What I could really have done with now was concrete, lots of it, and roads, flyovers, roundabouts, traffic lights, and thousands of buildings, stretching as far as the eye could see. I'd had enough of green stuff.

Mum wasn't the only one who seemed beyond happy with the place. Dad walked about beaming, as though he'd sunk a long putt, and Dexter ran around madly as if he was on hot coals. We unpacked the car and went into the cottage.

'You did well, Clive. This is so atmospheric,' said Mum, looking around, smiling, like some explorer unearthing an ancient dwelling.

I hoped she didn't like it too much. The thought of us moving somewhere as remote as this made me feel ill.

'Where's the TV?' asked Tallulah.

After a thorough search of the building Tallulah and I realised we were in a TV-free zone.

'There's no telly,' I said in my whiniest voice.

'We'll just have to make our own entertainment. Did you bring your books?'

'Who the hell reads books?'

'People with brains, Tyler.'

For me anything with more than five hundred words is too much like homework. I was so glad we were only staying here for four days.

I explored the cottage, which took about fifteen seconds, and only found two bedrooms. In my world, four into two definitely doesn't go.

'Mum, where's my bedroom?'

'You and Tallulah can share.'

The last time I shared with my sister was in Turkey about four years ago, and as far as I was concerned it was the last time. Not that I hate Tallulah, it's just that, apart from both being English and sharing the same address and parents, we have nothing in common.

'It's only for a few nights,' said Dad, who must have known all along that the place was one bedroom short of a house. 'Be good for you two to spend some quality time together.'

He was having a laugh. Quality time with my sister? Impossible.

Our bedroom was clearly built by people awaiting a growth spurt. The roof was so low I had to duck under the beams. I could almost touch both walls with my arms stretched. The two single beds took up every spare millimetre of space. It was less of a holiday cottage, more of a doll's house.

'Baggsy the bed by the window,' said Tallulah, leaping on to it.

'You're welcome,' I replied. It had a view of sheep. My bed had a view of wall. Much more interesting.

I'd moaned all summer long about our lack of holiday, but this was not what I had in mind. To me it's not a real holiday unless you get on a plane, and the place you land in is hotter than the one you left, and the people speak a language you don't understand, and there's a beach.

After I'd had a good long whinge about the cottage, the sleeping arrangements, and Wales in general, Mum and Dad said we were going for a walk. I like walking Dexter. It gives me a chance to unload my problems. I wasn't so keen on the idea of walking my parents. But this was deepest Wales. What else was there to do?

'Put your sun cream on,' said Mum.

'We're in Wales.'

'The sun doesn't discriminate.'

Better do than argue. For Mum, you can never be too safe. I dabbed a blob of factor thirty on my nose, put on the relevant footwear, and we set off.

'I hope this track leads somewhere interesting,' I said. 'Like a shopping centre, with burger bars and video games.'

'Don't be stupid.'

'There's no one here,' I said, scanning the horizon for signs of human life.

'Lovely, isn't it?' said Dad.

'If it was that lovely there'd be people about.'

Beaches are packed because they're great fun. The countryside is deserted because it's not great fun, and no one wants to go there. That's my theory anyway.

The talk on our walk got so small it almost disappeared, but as we reached the brow of yet another hill, the talk suddenly got big again.

'I wonder what happened to that girl in the woods,' puffed Mum.

Held my breath.

'Probably gone to the Caribbean with all the money she made from begging,' said Dad.

'Hope someone found her,' said Mum, resting against a rock.

My thoughts flew back to Ilkley. There'd been no calls from our neighbours or the police, so I guessed Spider hadn't gone into our house earlier than I'd told her. I hoped she waited until it was dark. Really dark. And fingers crossed she kept a low profile, sat on the floor, reading a book, not opening the windows for fresh air, hanging her clothes on the washing line, or wandering around like she owned the place. Problem was, I never quite knew with Spider. Could I have chosen a less reliable person to crash out in our house? Despite the sun beaming down, the thought made me shiver.

Having walked further than necessary, we turned around and headed back to the miniature house. Dad made a huge salad, which had more greenery than the Drivers' house. I hate salad. It's not what I'd call food, just brightly coloured bits of nothing that taste of air. Not like meat. Dad says we need to eat healthily once in a while. I wish it was once. But I kept my thoughts locked away. I'd moaned enough already today.

After clearing the dishes, washing up and looking at some sheep, I decided to go outside.

'Where you going, Tyler?'

'To the cinema.'

Neither Mum nor Dad smiled.

'Can't get a signal. I'm going up the hill.'

I grabbed my phone and headed up a stony track, illumined by an enormous moon. After a few hundred metres a tiny bar appeared on my screen. I decided against calling Spider. Didn't want the neighbours to hear the sound of Geordie drifting through their walls. I texted her instead.

Are u in yet?

A few seconds later came the reply.

In what?

Groan.

My house, I typed, somehow managing to omit the word, *idiot*.

All good. With smiley face.

You didn't set the alarm off?

No.

Thought it wouldn't hurt to remind her of the house rules.

Remember: no lights, no telly, no radio, don't go near front windows, don't make a mess, don't leave the house.

Smiley face.

Worried face.

Twenty-nine

'Been in touch with Michele?' said Mum, as I kicked my boots off at the door.

'Yeah.'

'How are things with this girl?' asked Dad, looking up from a dog-eared paperback.

Six eyes turned on me. Three brains looking for an answer. One tongue, horribly tied.

'Okay-ish.'

'You've gone red,' said Tallulah.

'It's sunburn.'

'So, nothing to report, then?'

'Correct.'

Realising that they weren't going to dredge up any more information on the Michele front, the conversation took a sharp left turn into Welsh tourism opportunities.

'I went online before we left. There's lots to do up here,' said Dad excitedly.

'Yeah, I hear *I Spy* is very popular in Wales.'

Gold medal for sarcasm.

Dad ignored me and continued, 'We can go up Mount Snowdon, the highest mountain in England and Wales. There's a big waterfall at Betws-y-Coed, and a lovely castle at Llandudno. There are also lots of farms we can go to.'

So far he'd failed to say anything of any interest whatsoever. But just when I thought I might actually die of boredom, Dad hit the jackpot.

'Or there's a giant zip wire at Penrhyn Quarry.'

'Yes.'

I take it back, Wales isn't just a lumpy green space. The zip wire turned out to be one of the best things I'd done all year. Having driven up to the quarry we got kitted out in all our flying gear. I love speed, and when I'm older I'm going to be a test pilot for jet planes, or failing that, move to Staines, so I can be near Thorpe Park.

The zip wire didn't fail to deliver. I was the first to go. Helmet on, suit on, strapped in, facing over a kilometre of excitement. Then I was off. It seemed the whole of Wales opened up before me, wind blasting my face, hurtling over the quarry far below, like an eagle chasing a very fast mouse. It was beyond amazing.

But no sooner had it started than it ended. I was followed down the wire by Dad, then Mum. Tallulah had to make do with the little dipper. She was a bit grumpy about that, but it's her fault for being seven. She loved it, though, and we both wanted to do it again, but Dad said we couldn't afford it. So we didn't.

'One less cupboard in the kitchen,' I pleaded.

'No.'

I think there should be zip wires everywhere, from the bathroom to the garden, from my bedroom to school, and maybe a really expensive one, from Yorkshire to London. It would cut down on pollution. It would make people happy. And it would create thousands of jobs in the zip-wire industry. I sometimes think I should run the country.

But the zip wire wasn't the only nice surprise that day. Being out of our hidden valley I received a message from Michele, make that several messages. She'd sent me a load of pictures from Crete, including one of her in that bikini. This photo would never be deleted. Whatever happened to us. She'd clearly forgiven me for anything she thought Spider and I had got up to.

Nice in Crete. Be even nicer if u were here. Several hearts. *You'd love the sea. Opposite of the lido.* Lots of laughing faces. *Can't wait 2 c u Ty.* An awful lot of 'x's.

I was warming again to Michele, in all parts of my anatomy. She'd sent a lovely text *and* a photo. What more could I want? And yet. And yet. And yet. There was the way she'd behaved at the café, how she'd treated Luke, what he'd had to say about her, and what she'd said about Spider.

Careful, Tyler, careful.

Wales is boring. But went on amazing zip wire. Awesome.
Lots of mad emojis.

How to finish the message?

Bye bye.

Delete.

Luuuurving the bikini.

Delete.

Can't wait till u r back.

Delete.

Good to catch up when u r back. Tx.

My finger hovered over 'Send'. Was it too much? Too
little? Should I change *'good'* to *'love'*? Should I change
'catch up' to *'do something'*? Should I alter *'u r back'* to
'we're together'? Was one 'x' enough? Don't think I'd ever
spent so long staring at eight words and two letters.

Damn it.

Send.

If I wasn't sure about her, did it matter if it wasn't
one hundred per cent perfect?

I decided to send a message to the other girl in my
life.

Everything ok?

Seconds morphed into minutes.

No reply.

The absence of a ping on my phone had me worried.
It wasn't as if Spider had a job or anything. All she had

to do was to sit around a house without being spotted. And she had a phone, a charger. So why hadn't she responded? Maybe she'd fallen asleep on the sofa. I hoped so.

On the way back to the doll's house I stared at the sheep and managed to get my pulse rate down. But no sooner was it down than Mum cranked it back up again.

'Just seen a message on Facebook,' said Mum, looking at her phone. 'There's been some burglaries in Ilkley.'

So much for escaping crime.

'Do you think I should get Vicky to check the doors and windows, and have a look in the house?'

I suddenly felt sick. Vicky was our next-door neighbour and general neighbourhood nosy person.

'You set the alarm, didn't you?' said Dad.

'Yes, but burglars are smart. They can overpower pretty much anything.'

This was beyond critical. Mum about to get a neighbour to check our house for anything strange. And Spider, in our house, undoubtedly behaving strange. Why didn't she answer her phone?

'Mum, can't you relax for once? You're on holiday.'

'Burglars don't take holidays.'

'What've we got that's worth stealing?'

'He's got a point,' said Dad. 'Apart from my golf clubs, there's nothing of value.' Mum sighed her disagreement at his remark. 'Anyway, if there was someone in our house Vicky would hear them.'

I wished he hadn't said that. I really wished he hadn't said that.

'Okay,' said Mum, switching her phone off. 'But if we get back and our house has been ransacked, you two are in for a world of pain.'

Thirty

Wish we'd saved the zip wire until last. Over the next few days none of my adrenaline was required. We took the little steam train up to the summit of Mount Snowdon. Unfortunately, we'd chosen one of those foggy mornings when all you could see were people walking around wondering where Wales had gone. I went into the shop at the top and took some pictures of postcards of the mountain, to show people what we'd been missing. I'd send them to Michele if she ever bothered to reply to me. I tried Spider again. No reply from her either.

But next day, on a trip to Conwy Castle, my luck returned. I found a quiet battlement and sent a text.

Spider?

What?

Where u been?

Shopping.

Hoped this was one of her jokes.

Back 2morrow. Sneak out in morning. V early.

Smiley face.

Is the house tidy?

Smiley face.

Meet u in woods when I'm back.

Smiley face.

Was sure that there was something I'd forgotten but couldn't think what.

Be careful.

Smiley face.

It was like communicating with a three-year-old.

We said goodbye to fields, hills and sheep and three hours later were saying hello to fields, hills and sheep. Yorkshire was like Wales, but with road signs that made sense.

Dad stopped the engine, Tallulah stopped her movie, and we climbed, stiff-legged, out of the car. Mum had heard nothing from neighbour Vicky, but it didn't stop me feeling nauseous with nerves.

Patron saint of house cleaning, please make Spider tidy the house, please.

'Home sweet home,' sighed Mum, as she stretched her arms and looked lovingly at Fairspew.

I helped Dad unload our stuff from the boot while Mum took out her keys and opened the front door. The second she did it, my mistake came up and hit me.

'Clive, you set the alarm when you left, didn't you?'

'Yes, always,' he said, a worried look on his face.

I'd forgotten to remind Spider to put the alarm on when she left. Crap. What else had Idiot Boy forgotten?

Ashen-faced, Dad dropped a bag and followed her inside. My breath was too scared to come out.

'What's up, Mummy?' said Tallulah, hurrying behind them.

'I don't know yet, honey.'

Dad dashed into the sitting room, looking round anxiously. 'The TV's still here, and the sound system.'

Mum had gone into the kitchen. 'There's a cup and a plate in the dishwasher. I emptied it before I left.'

Spider, you nutjob.

Dad followed her into the kitchen. 'Has anyone got a spare key?'

'No.'

'Keep looking,' said Dad.

I tried to think of something, anything, to get me out of this mess, but there was no lie big enough. Why hadn't I got out of the car first and dashed inside? I could have pretended to turn the alarm off. As they unpacked it would have given me the chance to look around for telltale signs of Spider. But it was way too late for that. Mum and Dad knew someone had been in the house.

I peeked in the front room and saw a long impression on the sofa, where Spider's body had been. I slumped into a chair, my head in my hands, listening to Mum clomping around upstairs, wardrobe doors and cupboard drawers opening and closing as she looked for signs of burglary.

'My toys are all here,' shouted Tallulah.

'And my golf clubs are still there,' exclaimed Dad, from the utility room.

'Clive,' screamed Mum.

I needed to go upstairs and see what all the fuss was about.

'How on earth could that have happened?' said Mum, holding a towel that was three times its usual weight, thanks to all the water it was holding.

Spider must have had a shower, and probably used the towel to mop the floor.

'At least nothing's been taken,' I said, trying to defuse the situation.

'That we know of. I should have rung Vicky,' said Mum, giving Dad and I the evil eye. 'We'd better call the police.'

The P word was like the blow you don't see coming. I felt myself going light-headed and held on tightly to the bathroom door frame for support.

'What are they going to do?' said Dad.

'Dust for fingerprints. Look for clues. Someone's been in our house, Clive.'

I had two possible courses of action. Both potentially catastrophic. Pretend I knew nothing about the mystery visitor and hope Spider's fingerprints weren't on any police database. Or come clean about Spider and beg for forgiveness. I decided that Option A had the most potential. Unless a neighbour had seen Spider it was unlikely they'd track her down. And surely the police had better things to do than look for burglars who'd forgotten to burgle anything.

I could finally breathe.

But my breathing didn't last long.

There was one more thing I'd forgotten to tell Spider about.

'Mummy, look at this,' said Tallulah, handing the front-door key to her.

Mum looked at it with ever-narrowing eyes. 'Where did you find this?'

'It was peeking out from under the front-door mat.'

I'd meant to tell Spider to throw the door key in the River Wharfe on her way back to the woods. But, no, she hadn't done anything that clever. She'd left it under the front-door mat. Someone must have kicked the mat when they came in. And my well-worked plan had suddenly stopped working.

Mum twisted the key over in her hand. 'Someone's had this cut.'

And then she turned to me.

'Tyler, do you know anything about this?'

Thirty-one

I had a split-second.

No more.

The lie was dressed up and ready to go out. *I've no idea how the key got there, Mum. Maybe I dropped mine by the front door.* But the truth was also desperate to escape, elbowing the lie aside to prove that he was the stronger of the two. *I lent it to the homeless girl.*

I knew that if the lie won, it would only be a temporary victory. There would be more telltale signs in the house, and the police would look into any odd characters in the area, like a bedraggled Geordie living in the woods.

'I had the key cut, Mum.'

I reckoned if I told them why I'd done it everything would be okay. I mean, helping people – isn't that what Mum does? Isn't that what everyone's meant to do?

'What the hell have you been up to?' she screamed.

I'd never seen Mum look so angry, her face screwed up tighter than a fist.

'Clive,' she shouted. 'Get down here.'

Heavy footsteps brought him breathless down the stairs.

'What's happened? Is something missing?'

'Not that I know of. But I think our son has something to tell us.'

'What's he done?' said Tallulah, joining the group.

'Go to your room,' instructed Mum.

'I want to know.'

'Go,' screamed Mum, at a volume that made Tallulah's lower lip wobble.

She trudged upstairs as Mum and Dad turned to confront me.

'In the sitting room.'

I walked in slow motion. Do prisoners ever walk fast to the execution chamber? The door slammed behind me. I slumped on the sofa. Mum and Dad stayed standing, arms folded, eyes blazing.

'What the hell's been going on?'

I knew they'd hate what I was about to tell them, but they'd hate me even more if I didn't tell them. And the sooner it was out, the sooner life could return to something like normal.

'I let the homeless girl stay here.'

The clock again.

Tick. Tock.

'You what?' exclaimed Dad.

'She had nowhere to stay.'

'You said you didn't know where she was,' shouted Mum, eyes bulging.

I looked down at the carpet. A blue hair-tie. Probably Spider's. More evidence. More mistakes.

'I knew you wouldn't let her stay.'

'You're bloody right there,' said Dad. 'Letting a tramp sleep in our house.'

'She's not a tramp.'

'So, what is she, businesswoman of the year? She's a bloody down-and-out. We'll have to get the entire place fumigated.'

Tick. Tock.

'Whose bed did she sleep in?'

'She slept on the sofa.'

'Have to get that cleaned too,' said Mum, sniffing.

'She's not a wild animal. She's a human being.'

'One who's been sleeping in the woods,' exclaimed Dad.

Mum got her inhaler out and took a large puff.

'She had nowhere to go.'

'So we turn this place into a bloody doss house,' said Dad, leaning against the mantelpiece and shaking his head.

I knew what he thought about people like Spider. But I hoped I'd find an ally in Mum.

'You stop people watching bad stuff online. You protect people. That's all I was trying to do.'

'She doesn't protect them by bringing them into our house.'

'He was talking to me, Clive.'

'Sorry for breathing,' said Dad, pacing the room, hands jammed deep in his pockets.

'I'm all in favour of helping people. But not like this.'

'Why didn't she go with those homeless charity people?' said Dad, at a volume Vicky would have no trouble hearing.

'Something bad happened to her in a hostel. She's scared.'

'So you decide to let her stay here, like some bloody Airbnb?'

Tick. Tock.

'And how well do you know her? Is she on drugs? Is she an alcoholic? Has she got HIV? She could have brought a whole gang of dossers into our house.'

'She had nowhere to go, Dad.'

'Suppose she's been scoffing our food as well,' he said. 'Probably polished off the drinks cabinet.'

Mum had stayed silent through Dad's rants, but I knew she wouldn't stay quiet for long. She sat down on the sofa next to me, clutching her inhaler.

Tick. Tock.

'Do you know the worst thing about this?'

No, but I've got a feeling you're going to tell me.

'You lied to us, Tyler. You lied to us.'

Thirty-two

I hoped that would be the end of it, that the storm, having hit, would move on, looking for another victim. But it wasn't over. Not by a long way.

'There are going to be repercussions,' said Dad. 'You've been an absolute bloody disgrace.'

Hated being spoken to like that. Hated them. Hated everything. My head slumped forward. Tears began to appear. Unlike Spider I had no glasses to catch them.

'Look around,' I cried. 'She hasn't done anything.'

'Even if she hasn't, you have,' said Mum.

But what exactly had I done? Let someone with no roof, have a roof. Someone with no food, have some food. Someone with nowhere to sleep, have somewhere to sleep. Someone with no shower, have a shower. How could that be so wrong?

'We're going to take any money you've saved to have this house cleaned from top to bottom.'

Bang go the headphones.

'All you care about is this stupid house,' I shouted. 'Carpets and cupboards mean more to you than people.'

'This is not how you help,' said Mum.

'So how do you help?' I said, looking up, tears clouding my vision. 'Do you volunteer? Do you work at a hostel? Do you give them food, money? No, you two do nothing.'

'That's not true,' intoned Mum. 'I spend day after day trying to stop evil people radicalising, poisoning, perverting. That isn't nothing.'

'So why do you hate me for doing something?'

They think they've got all the answers. But I know they don't.

Tick. Tock.

'You should have talked to us.'

'I did talk to you. Over dinner. You made it pretty clear what you thought of her. I even had to remind you to call the charity people.'

Mum looked like she did after a long session watching the evil stuff. She grabbed her inhaler and took another puff. *So much for fresh air*, I thought.

'This isn't for you to solve.'

'Your dad's right,' said Mum. 'You've got to leave this sort of thing to the experts.'

'But where are these experts now?' I said, looking under a cushion. 'If there are so many effing experts how come she's got no house, no money, no job?'

'I will not have swearing in this house.'

I'd had enough of them. *Fairview*. Where were their fair views? I got to my feet and made for the door. But I didn't reach it. Dad grabbed my arm tight.

'I haven't finished yet.'

'Piss off.'

Dad raised his fist.

'Clive, please, no.'

The fist disappeared. His breathing slowed.

'Give me your phone.'

'What?'

'You heard. Give me your phone.'

'I need it.'

'You do *not* need it. You've lied to your mother and father. You can have the phone back when you've proven to us you can be trusted.'

I took the phone out of my pocket and threw it away. It hit a picture frame and smashed the glass. A photo of us all on the London Eye. The fractured family.

'Tyler,' screamed Mum.

I broke free from Dad, stormed out of the room, slammed the door and ran upstairs. I fell on my bed and gave the pillow a massive punch. How could things have gone so completely and utterly wrong? I'd only wanted to earn a bit of money at the lido and look where it had got me. Anger welled up inside me like magma. They'd taken my phone as well as all the money I'd earned. For what? A lie? Yes, but not a terrible lie. It wasn't like I'd killed someone. And what had Spider done? Left a cup and plate in a dishwasher, a key on a front mat, a wet towel in the bathroom? From the way they were banging on you'd think she'd burned the house down.

But it wasn't just my parents I was angry with, it was Spider too. I'd told her over and over again to be careful, and what had she been – uncareful, or whatever the sodding word is. Maybe after living in a wood she wasn't used to tidying up after herself. Or maybe she thought it didn't matter. But she didn't know my mum. She could spot a crumb at fifty paces.

I lay there trying to decipher their mumbles. But I didn't need to. The mumbles soon turned into shouts.

'None of this would have happened if he had some friends up here,' went Dad.

'You're looking at me as though that's my fault.'

'You're the one who wanted to come up here. For a better life.'

'We both agreed on that, Clive. You're rewriting history. And I've tried everything to find him some mates. He won't listen to me. Won't listen to anyone.'

I'd never heard Mum and Dad shout at each other like this before. Not sure I wanted to ever hear it again. I needed to get away. I leaped from my bed and hurried downstairs to the front door.

'Where the hell do you think you're going?' said Dad, as he appeared, red-faced, from the sitting room.

I opened the door and hurried down the path.

'Come back here,' he shouted.

I started to run.

Heard footsteps behind me.

But they soon faded to nothing.

A hundred metres on I looked back. Dad had made a half-hearted effort to chase me, but golfers can't run. He stood, panting, holding on to a lamp post for support.

'Tyler,' he yelled.

Yell all you like, Dad.

I ran through Ilkley.

Next stop, Middleton Woods.

Thirty-three

I reached the V in the fence and waded through the ferns until I spotted the blue plastic sheet among the bushes, laden with leaves.

'Spider,' I shouted.

A head popped out from under the sheet and Spider got unsteadily to her feet. She looked tired, bedraggled, bits of foliage sticking to her clothes, like a failed attempt at camouflage.

'What's the marra?' she said, spotting my face was the opposite of happy.

'You're the matter. You left stuff in the house,' I said, struggling for breath.

'Like what?'

I paused to drag air into my lungs. 'Like the front-door key, dishes in the dishwasher, soaking wet towel in the bathroom. All the things I asked you not to do.'

'I left the key under the mat.'

'Well, someone must have kicked the mat, 'cos my sister found it.'

Spider swung at a twig with her muddy trainers. 'Sorry, man. Thought I'd been dead careful.'

'You were dead stupid. Why didn't you take the key with you?'

'Didn't knaa what to dee with it. Was gonna tell you where I hid it.'

Why hadn't I written it all down, like study cards?

'They know it was me?'

Nodded.

'And went mental?'

Nodded again.

'Sorry.'

I snapped a branch.

'They're gonna take all my holiday money to get the house cleaned.'

'It wasn't dirty.'

'And they've taken my phone.'

'Said I was sorry, man.'

Was going to take more than a couple of sorries to change how I felt.

'Any chance you could get a job? Pay me back.'

Spider's mouth flopped open and stayed flopped.

'You been on the wacky baccy? Do yous know how hard it is to find work? Proper work? Answer, bloody impossible. I've tried every shop and business in Ilkley.

They want an address, references, qualifications. All the things I haven't got. Look around, Tyler, what do you see? Gold bars, diamonds, suitcases bulging with money? I haven't even got a mirror for me make-up. Haven't even got any make-up.'

Birdsong filled in the silence we'd made.

'Why don't you try begging?'

Spider's face told me I shouldn't have said this, really shouldn't have said this. She slumped to the damp earth, as if my words had been bullets.

Wish I could go back in time and do this scene again. Once again I'd made a total balls-up. Mum and Dad had made me mad, and I'd gone and taken my madness out on the person who least deserved it. I should have taken Dex for a walk first. But too late now. I'd said it.

Now it was my time turn to say it.

'I'm sorry...'

'Shut the eff up, Tyler.'

'I could...'

'I said shut the eff up,' she screamed.

Silence drew a line under her scream. The only noise came from the distant barking of a dog. Even the birds had stopped tweeting now. The woods had eaten every other sound.

Spider finally turned her face on me, the paleness had gone, replaced by vivid red. Her mouth was twisted, her eyes squeezed close. 'You are one little bastard, Tyler. All I asked for were some swimming lessons. I didn't ask to stay in these effing houses. That was your stupid idea. And now because Mummy and Daddy have taken your money, you want me to go begging?'

Why had I said that word?

'You know what you need? A good punch in the face.'

I took a step back.

'Do you know what pride is? Did they ever teach you that word at school?' Nodded. 'Well, I haven't got much, but I've still got that. Me mam always said don't let anyone steal your pride.' She shook her head. 'Begging? Is that what you take me for, an effing beggar?'

'I said I was sorry.'

But she wasn't listening.

'Aye, people also inject themselves with needles, drink super-strength lager at ten in the morning, and take spice, which turns them into zombies. I'm not like them either. Believe it or not, I keep trying to make something of myself. Looking for jobs. Reading. Learning to swim. But what do you see? A total loser. Isn't that right?'

Shook my head.

'Answer me, Tyler.'

'No, you're not a loser.'

I stamped a fern into the ground. How had everything gone so ridiculously wrong?

'Don't care what yous think any more. You don't know the first thing aboot me. You don't know anything. You in your lovely little world, your lovely little town, saving for your headphones, hanging out with bikini-girl, moaning because you're not lying on some sodding beach in Spain. I have nothing, absolutely nothing. No mam. No dad. No proper dad. No friends. Nowhere to live. Think about that next time you complain 'cos you've got no pocket money.'

'Things aren't that great for me either.'

She laughed.

'Yes, they bloody are. I've spoiled your little world for a couple of days, maybe a week, until your mam and dad calm doon and your life gets back to normal. But my life is never getting back to normal. It never was normal. This is my life,' she said, looking at her sleeping bag, the plastic sheet and the woods.

'You might get another cleaning job.'

Spider snorted. 'How much do you think a cleaner earns? Any idea?'

Shrugged.

'Ask your mam, then ask her how much rent is. How much a weekly food bill is. Get your calculator out. Then come back and tell me the answer.'

I'd had enough. Spider was better than any teacher

at making me feel bad. Needed to get away. I turned and walked out of the woods. Too angry to say 'goodbye' or 'good luck'.

But Spider wasn't finished yet.

'If you want headphones that badly you could always try beggin'.'

Thirty-four

It was good to be back in the pool.

Away from everything.

Even the cold felt good.

Thanks to my season pass, swimming was about the only thing I could afford. My parents had taken sixty pounds off me to clean the house that didn't need cleaning. They might as well have burned it. It left me with barely enough for a set of earplugs. And it was nearly the end of the holidays. With fewer people going away it meant fewer lawns to mow, plants to water, cats to feed.

It was strange being back in the lido. Not long ago I'd been in this same water, teaching Spider how to swim. I'd thought she was weird at first. Then I realised that she was normal, with abnormal problems. And then I'd gone back to thinking she was weird again. But I only thought that because of what had happened. She'd been careless, but then so had I. Should have told Mum and Dad what

I planned to do. They'd have said no. But at least they'd have realised how serious I was about helping her. Then they might actually have done something, instead of just shouting at me and taking my money.

I still felt bad about asking her to go begging. I should have known from everything she'd said that Spider wouldn't do that. I'd wanted to help her, but instead I'd made her hate me. *You have an amazing talent, Tyler Jackson.*

I had mixed feelings about Spider going. She'd made me laugh. She'd filled a gap in my life. For a while, at least. She'd given me money. Some of it. She'd given me advice. But she'd also brought something I didn't need. Problems. Lots of them. Maybe she wanted me to experience a bit of her world, a place where nothing ever went right.

Pride. Isn't that what she'd talked about? Where was mine? I was proud of helping her, even though I'd failed. But I wasn't proud of what I'd said, how I'd made her feel. I guess when someone's got so little, it doesn't take much to make them feel worthless.

I didn't want to think about her any more, but some thoughts are unstoppable, no matter how hard you try to block them. I thought of where she was heading next. Leeds. A big place. Surely she'd find a job there. Then there was the cousin she was going to stay with. Hopefully this one was nice, with a kind partner, and would let her stay on her sofa for as long as she liked until she found her own place.

And then there was Michele.

Mum had let me look at my phone briefly. Michele had sent me a few more pictures. No bikini shots. Instead she was in T-shirt and shorts with her mum and dad, exploring the ruins of some old city called Knossos that looked like it had sustained heavy bombing. Didn't know she was into stuff like that. But then I still hardly knew her at all.

I wondered if she'd sent me pictures of the ruins as punishment. I also wondered if I should tell her what I'd done. She hadn't liked Spider, so maybe she'd be happy about what had happened. Or maybe she'd be angry. I could never quite tell what her reaction to anything might be.

Mum let me send Michele a message. Think she was happier me seeing a girl who had a home rather than a girl who didn't. She even gave me a fiver.

The day Michele got back we met in Costa.

Michele looked better than ever. She'd gone the sort of colour you see in sun-cream ads. Didn't think it was possible to change so much in such a short period of time, but Michele had managed it.

I went to kiss her cheek but she swivelled her head and got lips instead.

Felt good.

'I missed you,' she said.

'I missed you,' I said, sounding like a parrot.

I went to the counter and came back with a couple of smoothies, and a request for more money.

'You haven't got fifty p, have you? Bit more expensive than I thought.'

Bad start to the morning.

'Lucky I'm not after you for your money.' Michele just about managed to fit her hand in the pocket of her denim skirt and pull out a coin.

I gave the warm fifty p to the girl at the counter and returned to our table.

'You're brown,' I said.

'You're not,' she replied.

'What did you get up to?'

'Snogged half a dozen fit Greek boys. Got off with the water-ski instructor. Usual stuff.' I gave one of my crocodile laughs. 'I am joking.'

'Knew that.'

'You?'

'Went to Wales.'

'I know you went to Wales, you clart 'ead.'

'Er, walked up lots of hills and stuff, but the best part, by a trillion miles, was the zip wire in Penryhn Quarry. Beyond awesome. I was so revved up for it. You go flying over the quarry. I went over a hundred miles an hour, or it could have been kilometres…'

'That's enough about the zip wire, Ty.'

Michele took my hands, stared deep into my eyes and smiled. She looked like an angel, a brown angel.

I decided it was time to tell her.

'Did something a bit stupid while you were away.'

Michele let go of my hands and leaned forward, anticipation lighting her face. I took a big slurp to gather myself.

'You know that homeless girl?'

'The fake homeless girl.'

Michele's face was now a little more serious, a little less attractive. Wondered whether it was too late to change the subject. I could say, 'Well, she's left town.' To which Michele would say, 'So what exactly is the stupid thing you did?' And I'd be so tied up in knots I'd have to feign a vomiting bug and dash to the toilet and stay there until Michele had forgotten what I'd said or gone home.

I'd passed my lie-by date.

'I let her stay in my house.'

'You did what?' she shrieked.

Heads turned in our direction. Ilkley wasn't a shrieky sort of place.

'She had nowhere to stay, so I let her sleep on our sofa.'

'And your parents were okay about that?'

'No. I didn't tell them. But they found out.'

Michele leaned back in her chair, as if the weight of my news was too heavy and about to tip her over. The chair returned to four legs.

'What on earth did you hope to gain by that?'

'Gain? It wasn't for me to gain anything. It was for her.'

'So,' she said, knitting her brown fingers together tightly, 'she gets to sleep at your place, but when we had a whole house to ourselves you couldn't wait to get rid of me.'

'It's not like that.'

'What is it like?'

'She's homeless. You're not.'

'Oh, yeah, panic attacks one minute, homeless the next. She'll have a brain tumour by the end of the week.'

The old Michele was back.

'She was sleeping under a bush in Middleton Woods. You don't do that for fun.'

'You do if you're an attention-seeker. Sounds the type who'll do anything to get what she wants.'

'And what exactly does she want?'

'You.'

The reunion couldn't have gone much worse.

Michele was still jealous of Spider, even though I'd done nothing to foster this jealousy. If I did have the hots for her, would I really admit to letting her stay at my house? Would I even breathe a word about her? Absolutely not.

But Michele didn't see the world through ordinary eyes. It would have been easier to deflect a meteorite than get her off the subject. I was even prepared to talk about Ancient Greek ruins. Anything but this.

'Tell me about Knossos.'

'No. I can't believe you let her do that.'

'Michele, she's gone.'

'But not from your mind. You're still thinking about her.'

'No, I'm not.'

'Well, you're talking about her. How can you talk about her and not think about her?'

'I'm not going to give her a second more of my attention.' Michele frowned, clearly not believing a word. 'If I had my phone I'd show you my pictures are the ones you sent me. There's not a single one of her.'

'Because you've downloaded them on to your laptop.'

'She's gone to stay with her cousin in Leeds. I'm never going to see her again.'

Michele's brow looked like a crinkle-cut crisp. 'I don't like being messed around. You know that.'

Only too well.

Michele went quiet for a bit and sucked on her smoothie.

'Just want things to work out between us,' she said, staring at me. 'I like you, Ty. I like you a lot.'

Glad there was one person on the planet who appreciated me.

'Thanks.'

She took my hands and leaned forward.

'Have you still got the key to that house with the cats?'

Thirty-five

• • •

The sky was wall-to-wall blue as Dexter and I made our way past Ilkley Tarn and up the path on to the high moor. It was good to be with a creature who truly loved you, who didn't have a critical word to say about you, and who would never leave you. Dexter seemed perfectly happy with his current home. I guess a hill's a hill, a field's a field to him. I can't imagine him lying in his basket at night thinking, *I quite like West Yorkshire, but I prefer the gradients in Wales.*

If only I could be happy with my lot.

There was no reason I shouldn't be. As Spider reminded me, I had a nice house. Small, but it had walls and a roof and a bed. My parents no longer wanted to have me killed and turned into pig feed. I had a girl who liked me. And I still had twenty-three pounds eighty sitting in my bedside cabinet.

But something was nagging me. Make that someone.

'What do you think happened to Spider?'

Dexter nosed around in the dirt.

'Not spiders.'

Dexter looked at me, ears standing to attention, tongue lolling.

'You think she's landed a job on a hundred grand a year with a company car?'

Dexter ran off, clearly thinking I'd gone mad.

I'd tried and failed to forget about the homeless Geordie. I'd invested so much time and effort into helping her, it was hard to walk away as if nothing had happened. I wanted to know she was okay. She'd said some cutting things, but then I guess I'd said some pretty bad stuff about her. I didn't want things to end the way they had in Middleton Woods. It was like watching a film where the hero disappears. I wanted a better ending. And I had an idea how to get one.

My parents still had my phone, so I couldn't call or text Spider, but I thought of a way to find out how things were going in Leeds. There was someone in Ilkley who would know the cousin she was staying with. I took Dexter home, and headed through town. But as I neared my destination my heart began pounding. What was I doing this for? For Spider's sake or mine? Would it really help me to stop thinking about her? All I was sure was that I had to know.

I stood at the rusting metal gate.

Chrissie had been horrible to me the last time I was

here. But I guess I'd tricked my way into her house. Maybe she'd be friendlier this time.

Come on, Tyler, are you a man or a mouse?

Man-boy Tyler opened the gate and strode purposefully towards the front door.

Knock. Knock.

A few moments later I heard the sound of shuffling slippers on lino. The door opened to reveal a shocked-looking Chrissie.

'You again?' she snarled.

Swallowed hard.

'Wondered if you knew what happened to Spider?' I said, fear making my words come out strange.

'You've got some bloody cheek coming back here.'

'Who is it?' boomed a man's voice from somewhere in the house.

'Delivery.'

'Put wood in t'hole,' he bellowed. 'You're letting t'draught in.'

Chrissie stepped outside and pulled the door close behind her, leaving the smallest gap you could have without actually shutting it. She looked as nervous as I felt.

'She told me she'd gone to her cousin's in Leeds.'

Chrissie gave a smoker's laugh, one that was fifty per cent cough.

'Told you that, did she? Full of rubbish, that girl.

She hasn't got a cousin in Leeds. Hasn't got a cousin anywhere, apart from here. Her mam had one brother. He had one child, me.'

Why would Spider pretend to have a cousin she didn't have?

'She doesn't have any relatives in Leeds?'

'Na. Hasn't even been to Leeds, as far as I know.' She looked at her feet. There was a toe sticking out where slipper should have been. 'Was a bit harsh on the bairn.'

Didn't know much Geordie, but I knew this much – bairn means kid.

'Did you call her a bairn?'

'Aye.'

'She's eighteen, isn't she?'

Chrissie shook her head.

'Na, Spider's sixteen.'

Thirty-six

Sixteen.

Only a year older than me. I'd convinced myself she was eighteen. On the basis of what? She looked it. She was tall. She had a tattoo. I'd never asked her. Never looked at anything with her date of birth on it. No wonder she was finding it so hard to find work. You can't get a job at sixteen, not a good one. You have to be an apprentice or a trainee stacking shelves at Tesco. You'd never get enough to get a house. Not even a flat. Not even a shed. Not at that age.

'Are you sure?'

''Course I bloody am. She's me cousin, isn't she?'

Sixteen.

I couldn't get the number out of my head. But it seemed I wasn't the only one whose head was being messed with.

'Should never have let him throw her oot,' she said, looking back at the house. 'I'm the only family she's got here. Some family I turned out to be.'

But before she could utter another word the front door opened wide to reveal a big, bearded guy in gym vest and sweatpants. Guessed it was Chrissie's boyfriend, the one who didn't want Spider taking up all his sofa.

'What tha 'eck's goin' on't here?' he said, in as broad a Yorkshire accent as you'll find in Ilkley.

'Just a lad looking for jobs.'

His eyes shifted from me to Chrissie.

'Tha's tekking the mick. Said it were delivery.'

Chrissie looked scared as the big guy towered over her.

'Must have misheard.'

'Nowt wrong with my hearing. Your bloody accent more like.'

Not the time to ask any more questions about Spider.

'Better be off.'

'Aye, there's no jobs here,' he said. 'Ya cheeky tyke.'

'Bye,' I said.

No bye came back.

I walked down the path and turned to see the man grab Chrissie by the arm and pull her inside. A second later the door slammed. Hoped I hadn't got Chrissie into trouble. All I'd done was ask her about Spider. She's the one who'd made up the delivery story.

I trudged home, going over in my head what Chrissie had said. Why would Spider tell me she had a cousin in Leeds when she didn't? Maybe she wanted me to think she was okay. But why would she tell me that when she wasn't? Perhaps she just wanted me out of her life and was prepared to make up relatives to achieve it. Whatever the reason, I couldn't stop thinking about that number – sixteen. No wonder Spider walked the streets at night, too scared to go to sleep. That's why she was too frightened to go back into a hostel, and why she had panic attacks. Just a bairn.

Things must have been terrible for her to leave home that young. Maybe she wasn't even sixteen then, maybe fifteen, same age as me now. Spider seemed to be getting closer to me by the minute. Although I'd fallen out with Mum and Dad, I couldn't imagine falling out with them badly enough to feel forced to leave home and live on the street or jump from sofa to sofa.

Seeing Chrissie was meant to put an end to the story, but she'd gone and restarted it. Spider was still out there. In more trouble than ever. I walked into Fairspew, my head as messed up as it's ever been.

Mum was watching TV in the kitchen.

'Where've you been?'

'For a walk.'

'Without Dexter?'

'Walked him enough.'

Mum stared at me as I took off my trainers.

'Is everything okay, Tyler?'

When was the last time everything was okay? Over a year ago, when I was in London, my friends on tap, Brentford on a winning streak, and planning to go on holiday to Spain. Everything was good. The opposite of now.

'Yeah, okay,' I said, with no enthusiasm whatsoever.

'Sit down.'

I parked myself at the kitchen table next to her. Mum grabbed the TV remote and turned the volume down. She put her hand on mine.

'When you do a bad thing, the most important thing is that you learn from it. We don't like having to punish you.'

'Well, don't, then.'

Couldn't resist that one.

Even Mum mustered a smile.

'You need to look forwards, not backwards. Moving here hasn't been easy for your dad and I either.'

First time I'd heard her say that.

'His work's tough, tougher than he imagined. And I'm going to look for a new job.'

'Doing what?'

'Don't know. But I can't do this any more.'

I squeezed her hand.

'And we're trying hard to make new friends. But it's not easy for us, Tyler.'

It was the first time I'd felt sorry for my mum in a

long, long time. I thought everything had been perfect for them. Maybe she was too embarrassed to admit they'd made a mistake, like when people come back from holiday and pretend it was great, even though it rained every day and they all got food poisoning.

'You still think about that girl in the woods, don't you?'

Nodded.

'I know you felt something for her. And I while I don't condone what you did, I understand why you did it.'

Was good to hear Mum speaking like this for a change. Instead of having a go at me.

'But you've got to move on. She's gone.'

I looked up at the TV. An advert came on.

For sofas.

Thirty-seven

It was as though Spider had taken her sleeping bag and moved into my head. No matter how hard I tried I couldn't get rid of her. Why had she told me such a huge lie? Probably the same reason she didn't want to become a beggar – pride. She didn't want me to think she was a total loser. Wanted me to think she was okay, could stand on her own two feet. So she'd invented the cousin who didn't exist.

Did she do that for her benefit or mine? No idea. All I did know was that I was worried for her. She'd said in no uncertain terms she'd never go back to Tyneside. Instead she'd gone to Leeds, with no home, no job and no money. And the icing on the cake. Sixteen years old.

I so wanted to tell my parents, but Mum had already told me to forget about Spider, and Dad couldn't have made his feelings any clearer. Speaking to Michele would be a waste of words. Could tell my teachers, but school wasn't back for another week. But then an idea paid a visit. There's a charity shop that sells stuff for the homeless. Someone there might know what to do.

I walked up the Grove and into the shop, which, thankfully, was quiet. I spotted a girl on the till and summoned up the courage to speak.

'Excuse me, a friend of mine is homeless. She's gone to Leeds but doesn't know anyone. Wondered if you knew what I could do.'

The girl looked at me blankly. 'I'm volunteering for my Duke of Edinburgh Award. Got no idea.'

A small skin-fire broke out on my face.

'But Mrs Williams might be able to help.'

She called for Mrs Williams, and a few seconds later a smartly dressed middle-aged woman came bustling in from the back of the shop.

'Yes?'

'This lad here wants to ask about some homeless girl or something.'

I backed away from the till towards a shelf of faded paperbacks. Didn't really want anyone else to hear what I had to say. The woman looked at me expectantly.

'A friend of mine is homeless and she's gone to Leeds but doesn't know anyone there.'

'I see,' said the woman, nodding thoughtfully at my words. 'Well, there are quite a few homeless charities in Leeds. How old is she?'

'Sixteen.'

Her eyebrows turned into arches.

'That's very young. Can you tell me about her?'

I described Spider, down to the last swirl on her inky-blue arm.

'I'm only a volunteer here. But I'm sure one of the charities will come across her sooner or later.'

'And what will they do?'

'I guess they'll put her in a hostel.'

Not what I wanted to hear.

'What about a flat?'

'Not sure about that. I'm not really an expert on this sort of thing. I only work here on a Tuesday.'

'Thanks.'

On the way out, I spotted a leaflet about the homeless. Read it. Wished I hadn't. Said there were over 300,000 homeless people in Britain, and that homelessness was on the rise. More young people than ever were sofa surfing. Problem was, Spider didn't even have a sofa to surf on.

Then it got even darker.

Over four hundred people die on the streets every year. That meant someone had died today. Tomorrow it would be someone else's turn. Deaths were caused by violence, drug overdoses, illnesses, suicide and murder. Said that women who are rough sleepers can end up being trafficked into the sex trade. It made me feel sick.

On the plus side, the leaflet said there were loads of charities and groups doing stuff, paying close attention to people like Spider, young vulnerable girls who'd be referred to social services. Said there are foyers where young people can stay. Just one problem. Spider didn't want a foyer, not after what had happened to her. What did charities do then? Drag them there? Leave them on the street and hope they change their mind? Get the police to arrest them? The leaflet didn't say anything about that.

I left the shop and walked home, thinking. What if the charity people didn't find Spider in time? What if something terrible happened to her?

I needed to go to Leeds.

Thirty-eight

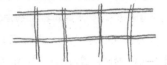

I'd only been to the city a few times, but apart from being the home of Leeds United and the Royal Armouries Museum, all I knew was that it was big. Not a great start. There must be a million doorways there. How on earth would I find the one with Spider curled up inside? I needed to speak to a homeless charity that knew the places rough sleepers go.

I googled a Leeds charity called Simon on the Streets. Their website said all the right things: *We provide support for those that either refuse to engage or who find it difficult to engage with other services. We concentrate on supporting entrenched rough sleepers and the rootless community that often finds itself street homeless.*

Sounded like they were talking about Spider, someone who needed help, but wouldn't ask for any. Bet they could tell me the sort of places I might find her.

But that was only the first phase of the plan. There was another slightly trickier one: getting to Leeds. I'd be gone for most of the .day. What would I tell my parents? Could say I was going to the lido, but nobody can survive in freezing water for that long. I could use Michele as an excuse. Mum would fall for that. But knowing Michele she'd turn up just after I'd left saying, 'Have you seen Tyler?' It would be like coming back from Wales, only worse.

I finally came up with a plan.

'Mum, Jack's asked me over to his for the day to hang out,' I said, as casually as I could.

She turned her quizzical eyes on me. 'How did he ask you over? We've got your phone.'

'Sent an email.'

No one in class ever sends emails. At least not to each other. But she's not to know that.

'What day was he thinking of?'

'Tomorrow.'

'Bit short notice.'

'Jack's busy. It's the only day he can squeeze me in.'

'Where does he live?'

'Blubberhouses.' Whoever named this village was clearly upset about something.

'How are you going to get there? Dad needs the car.'

For once the fact we were a one-car family came in handy. Mum wouldn't be able to drive me there. Nor could she come and pick me up.

'I'll get the bus. Jack said his mum will bring me back.'

Mum nodded, seemingly happy enough with this arrangement. But you can never tell for sure.

'Okay,' she said. 'Go and enjoy yourself. But be careful.'

I woke up with a bad case of butterflies.

Not sure why I was so nervous. I was only going to Leeds for the day.

Ate as much cereal as I could force down, put my coat on and headed for the door. But I'd barely touched the handle when Mum appeared.

'Let me give you a hug.'

She came over and squeezed me hard, as if I was a stress ball. I gave her a small squeeze back. Mum was being unnaturally nice. Decided to take advantage of this rare display of affection.

'Mum, is there any chance I could have my phone back?'

She looked at me as if I'd just asked for a yacht.

'Might need it to call you. In case of an emergency.'

'This is part of your punishment.'

'But I'll still be punished when I hand it back. Just for a few hours.'

I prayed Dad hadn't taken my phone to work with him.

Prayer answered.

Mum went to her handbag and slowly pulled out my phone as if she was handling a bomb. I went to grab it, but she pulled it away. 'I'll give you your phone on two conditions. You hand it straight back when you return, and you don't breathe a word of this to your dad.'

'Deal.'

She gave me the phone.

'Thanks, Mum.'

I don't often kiss her, but she deserved one today. Gave her a peck on the cheek.

'Have a great day.'

'Yeah.'

Grabbed my jacket and hurried outside before she changed her mind. So glad to have my phone back. I switched it on. Only fifty per cent charge. But enough for what I needed. I went through my contacts until I came to Spider and tapped away.

'The number you are trying to call is not reachable.'

I pressed the red button and tried again.

'The number you are trying to call is not reachable.'

I switched the phone off and carried on walking. *Not reachable.* What the hell did that mean? Not a good start to the day.

I hurried towards the bus stop, but I'd gone no more than fifty paces when a voice anchored me to the pavement.

'Ty.'

What had I done to deserve this?

'Oh, hi, Michele,' I said.

'Where you off to?'

Give me a break.

'Spending the day with Jack in Blubberhouses.'

From her expression you'd think I was emigrating.

'So, he means more than me?'

Why was it always so difficult talking to Michele?

''Course he doesn't, but haven't seen him all summer.'

Which was actually true.

'Thought we could spend the day together. Why didn't you tell me?'

'My parents have taken my phone.'

'So what's that in your pocket?'

Crap.

'Mum just gave it back to me, for today. We can meet up tomorrow,' I said, desperate to put an end to this.

Michele folded her tanned arms and scowled. 'Why do you keep lying to me, Ty?'

'I forgot I had it.'

'Strange, because I saw you using it a second ago. Who were you calling?'

'Jack.'

Michele, the human lie-detector, continued to stare. 'Why can't I come with you?'

'Jack and I will be playing video games pretty much all day. It'll be really boring. For you.'

'No more boring than hanging around here.'

'And he's got a very small bedroom.'

'You could play in the sitting room.'

She was unstoppable.

'His mum's probably only got food in for me and Jack.'

'I don't eat much.'

Enough, Michele!

'I'm gonna have to go.'

'Can I at least walk with you to the bus stop?'

My departure was not going well. It looked like I was going to have to get on a bus to Blubberhouses, where she thought I was going, then get off again at the next stop and get the bus back to Ilkley to get the bus to Leeds where she thought I wasn't going.

'It's a walk, Ty. I'm not asking you to run.'

'I'm fine, Michele, really fine.'

But just when I thought I was going to have to catch a bus I didn't want, she finally let me off the hook.

'All right, but the minute you're back I want you to call me, okay?'

'Okay.'

She came up close and pressed her body and her lips hard against mine. I instantly began to doubt the wisdom of my plan. I was going to Leeds to look for a girl who'd sworn at me and never wanted to see me again, when I could be spending the day locking lips with one who seemed infatuated with me.

'See you later, Ty.'

'Yeah.'

I waited until Michele had disappeared around a corner before heading off. I walked quickly to Ilkley station where the bus left, checking for anyone else who might want to stop me. But the streets were quiet. The shoppers still inside making lists. The tourists yet to descend. I climbed aboard the X84, paid the driver and went upstairs.

There were only three other people on the top deck. Probably not much going on in Leeds today. I found a seat near the back. There was a young couple sitting a few rows in front. She was leaning into him as if they were going around a bend. A few rows in front of them was an older man, head down, mumbling to himself or to a phone I couldn't see.

A few minutes later the engine started, and we moved off. It was over an hour to Leeds. Plenty of time to think about the day ahead. I knew it wouldn't be easy finding Spider, but it wasn't impossible either. Not like she'd be in a crowd or a busy shop. She'd be in a doorway or on a park bench, like the homeless I'd seen in Leicester Square or Piccadilly Circus. Never used to give them a second thought. Just people conked out, with a paper cup and a cardboard sign: *Homeless. Hungry. Please help. Thank you. God bless.*

When I was little, Mum or Dad would grab my hand and pull me past them, fast, as though they were about to jump up and stab me or something. I never thought I'd get to actually know someone like that, and find out what they're really like. Spider wasn't a danger. She was *in* danger.

I'd go to the Simon on the Streets charity first. Get some advice, and find the places homeless people hang out. That would narrow things down a bit. And then I'd start looking. But what if I found her? She'd already said she didn't want to go to a hostel. And I'd run out of houses in Ilkley for her to stay in. My best bet was to get her to talk to these Simon people. If they were experts they'd know what to do.

I looked again at the older guy on the bus. He was shabbily dressed, his hair sticking out in all directions. He didn't look as if he was going to work. Wondered if he was homeless. I guess that's the sort of thing homeless people do, stay on buses, and go round and round the same route all day long. To stay safe and warm. Until tomorrow. And start the whole thing over again.

If Spider had decided to do that, I'd never find her.

Prayed I was wrong.

I looked out of the window. The rolling fields of West Yorkshire had been replaced by concrete. We were on the outskirts of Leeds. Wouldn't be long before we reached the bus station. I stared through the glass. Tyler Jackson looked back at me. But he wasn't the Tyler Jackson I'd seen a couple of hours ago in the bathroom mirror. Smiley, hopeful. This one looked dead scared.

Houses swiftly gave way to offices, shops and pubs. The bus swung into the City Bus Station. Time to move. I jumped to my feet, hurried down the aisle, and clomped downstairs. I clutched the pole tightly as the bus pulled into its space. My breathing was short, sharp, as if I'd run the four hundred metres. No idea why I was so nervous. Just was. Suppose that's what happens to Spider with her panic attacks. They leap out of nowhere and get you.

The driver pressed a button, the doors swooshed open and I stepped into the bus station, head swivelling, as if I might spot Spider.

Not that lucky.

So busy looking I walked in front of a turning bus.

A horn blared.

Careful, Tyler, careful. Only been in Leeds ten seconds and nearly been run over.

I hurried around a corner and into a wall of stomach.

'What the chuffin' hell…'

'Sorry.'

My heart was going crazy, as if I was racing up Ilkley Moor with Michele. All I saw were people I didn't know. I felt they were watching me, wondering why I was standing there, like a postbox. What had seemed like a good idea now seemed the opposite.

I saw a sign in a shop window: *Welcome to Leeds.*

Thirty-nine

Whatever confidence I'd felt had dug a tunnel and escaped. Needed to get my plan back on track. First stop: Simon on the Streets. I'd written their address down, and with the help of one of those big city maps, found where I needed to go. It was a long way from the bus station, the other side of the River Aire, a part of Leeds I'd never been before. Reckoned I'd be doing enough walking today. Decided to call them instead.

'Hello, Simon on the Streets,' said a cheery young woman.

'Hi, my name's Tyler. Wonder if you can help me?' I said, trying hard to hide my nerves.

'Go ahead, Tyler.'

Swallowed as I got the story ready in my head.

'It's about a girl, a Geordie girl. She's been sofa surfing. Got thrown out of her cousin's flat in Ilkley and now she's gone to Leeds. She hasn't got any friends or family here. And hardly any money.'

'How old is this girl?'

'Sixteen.'

'Sixteen,' she repeated, in a voice without a sliver of surprise.

'You get homeless people that age?'

'Too many, I'm afraid.'

Never knew that. Most of the homeless I'd seen were adults. But I guess there must be young ones out there too, like Spider, surfing from house to house. Or hiding away somewhere.

'The girl's called Spider.'

'Spider,' she repeated, as though it was the most normal name in the world. 'Can you describe this girl?'

I painted a picture of Spider.

'And what was she wearing?'

'A blue sweatshirt hoody, jeans full of holes, white trainers, but not that white any more. And she had a green rucksack, with a black sleeping bag.'

Pause.

Reckon she was writing this all down.

'Do you have any health or risk concerns regarding her?'

'She can swim, so drowning's not a risk. But she gets panic attacks.'

'I see,' said the woman. 'Do these happen regularly?'

'Only saw one, when her cousin spat on her head at the lido. But it was really bad. She blacked out.'

'Is she on any medication or does she have any other health concerns?'

'Not that I know of.'

'Has she got a phone?'

'Yeah, but I can't get through.'

'I'll take it anyway.'

I gave her the number.

'Can you tell me anything about Spider's home life? Are her parents aware of her situation? Have they informed the police or social services?'

Like being in school. Doing an exam you haven't studied for.

'No. Her mam's dead. Doesn't like her dad. Doubt he'd have rung anyone. Don't think he's bothered about her. Never met him.'

'I see. And why was she staying at her cousin's?'

'She wanted to help Spider, but then changed her mind. Her boyfriend wanted his sofa back and they booted her out.'

Another pause.

'Do you know where she might be?' I asked.

'I'm afraid not.'

'Any suggestions?'

'Sorry. Even if we knew where Spider was we're not at liberty to disclose that.'

'Why?'

'For her own safety.'

Guess they thought I might not be a real friend. Could be an imposter. Someone out to harm her. Like you get online.

'Can you ring me if you find her?'

'I'm sorry, Tyler. Confidentiality is key in situations like this. But if we find Spider we'll ask her if it's okay to pass on a message that she's all right.'

'Thanks.'

I gave her my number. Just hoped Mum and Dad still didn't have my phone if Simon on the Streets called. That could take some explaining.

'So what happens now?'

'Hopefully one of the outreach workers will come across her, and a support plan will be put together.'

'What if she won't agree to this plan?'

'A sixteen-year-old girl on her own, sleeping rough, is very vulnerable. If she's been on the streets before she'll know it's not a good place to be. I'm sure she'll agree to whatever plan is put in place.'

'She won't go in a hostel. She was in one once. Something bad happened.'

'I'm sure the outreach workers will be able to help your friend.'

They'd have to be very persuasive.

'I'm in Leeds now. Can you give me a clue, even a little one, where I can start looking for her?'

'How old are you?'

'Fifteen.'

'I think it's best if you go home and leave that to us. Thanks for telling me about Spider. We'll do what we can. Nice talking to you, Tyler.'

Forty

* * * *

Guess I should have taken her advice and gone home. Left it to the experts. But they'd said the same about swimming. And what happened? I'd taught Spider to swim. Maybe I could go one better and find Spider before the outreach people did. After all, I knew her far better than them.

I scanned the street. People were hurrying in all directions, with lots to do. I was looking for someone who wasn't hurrying, with nothing to do. But where to start? The last twenty minutes of the bus journey had been all Leeds. The place was nowhere near as big as London, but still massive. Spider could be anywhere. Decided to go for a walk, my favourite summer pastime.

I left the shopping district and found myself in the sort of street you wouldn't expect to spot homeless people. Nice houses, big cars, tidy gardens. If a homeless girl rocked up here the owners would come out with a brush and shoo her away. But I had a look. Just in case.

Nothing.

But then up ahead I saw a church. As I got nearer I saw which type – a Catholic one. I'm not a fan of any particular god, but remembered when I lived in Chiswick homeless people would hang about the big church on the high road.

Decided to take a closer look.

Churches often have big grounds with trees and benches and graveyards where you could sleep. Not this one. The front garden was all concrete. I tried the door, but it was locked. I needed somewhere bigger, like a cathedral. Leeds is a city so it had to have one somewhere. I saw an old woman stooped over, dragging a tiny shopping trolley. More like a purse on wheels. She looked the type who did a lot of kneeling. I hurried over to her.

'Excuse me, do you know where Leeds Cathedral is?'

'What?' she said, angling her head up to me.

'Leeds Cathedral,' I shouted. 'Do you know where it is?'

'Yes, off Great George Street.'

'Where's that?'

'Over there,' she said, with a dismissive wave of her arm. 'About a mile.' And she scuttled off, without so much as a smile.

I headed in the direction of her wave, back towards the city centre, checking up alleys, behind wheelie bins, over hedges, but saw no one. Then, in among all the grey, I spotted a flash of green, as if a field from Ilkley had been dug up and deposited smack bang in the middle of Leeds. A park, definitely a place where homeless people would go. This one was called 4 Park Square. Sounded dead posh, and the buildings surrounding it looked expensive, but still worth a look. There weren't many people about, a couple of mums with matching baby buggies, a guy in a suit followed by a big vaping cloud, a jogger moving in slow motion, a group of teenage girls lying on the grass soaking up the last dregs of summer sun. But no one who looked remotely homeless.

I'd nearly done a full lap of the park when up ahead I saw a man on a bench, slumped. Slumped was good. Slumped meant he'd taken drink or drugs or was shattered from lack of sleep. I hurried towards him and saw he wasn't dressed in his Sunday best, wearing a dirty grey jacket, army trousers and muddy black boots. Most of his face was overgrown with beard, but what remained was mottled and red. If he had a home this man wasn't making the best use of it.

'Excuse me.'

The grizzled head turned in my direction. 'What je want?'

He was from Scotland.

'I'm looking for a girl.'

'Aren't we all?'

The man grinned, revealing a set of teeth no dentist had ever seen.

'Have you come across a girl, sleeping out? She wears glasses. Tall.'

'Tall glasses?'

'No, she's tall. The glasses are normal size.'

The man rubbed his beard. 'Think I need glasses.'

Sigh.

'And she's got tattoos down one arm. Not the other.'

'Tattoos doon one arm?' he said, mulling. 'What does the tattoo say?'

'*Mam.*'

'Think I saw a wee lass like that.'

'You did?' I said, my heart racing. 'Where?'

'Dundee. 2014.'

The Scotsman was very pleased at this and showed me his misshapen teeth again.

'Dinna see many lassies on the streets, wee fella. It's a man's game. You'd be mad to be oot here. Aye, mad as a ferret, like me.' And his beard vibrated as he laughed.

'Thanks a lot,' I said, backing away.

'You haven't got some spare change? Could dee with a brew.'

I scrabbled in my pocket and handed over twenty pence.

'Couldne buy a bottle of fresh air with that,' he said, screwing up his bulbous nose as he looked at it.

'Sorry,' was all I could think to say.

He put the coin deep inside his pocket, where no one could steal it, and went back to slumping.

Forty-one

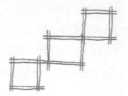

I headed further into the city, past the station, and down Boar Lane, my eyes darting in all directions. I spotted people in sleeping bags crashed out in doorways, others sat on the pavement with little handwritten cards. But none of them looked anything like Spider.

On the corner of Boar Lane and Briggate I saw a group of men who were totally out of place among the well-dressed locals. Their clothes looked older than me. On top of that they were loud and menacing. After what had happened in the hostel, I couldn't imagine Spider mixing with a bunch like that. I decided to give them a wide berth.

I walked up Briggate, my head swivelling about. The precinct was full to bursting with shoppers, laden with bags. Strange to see people buying clothes and stuff in the same street as others who haven't even got a pillow. No one paid the homeless any attention. As though they were invisible.

I turned left out of Briggate and found something on the pavement I didn't expect to see. *Tour de France. Grand Depart. Start. 5 July 2014.* The people who run the Tour must have got bored with France and decided to start it in Leeds, the least hilly city you could think of. I suppose it gave the cyclists a bit of a rest. I wondered if Spider had managed to get her hands on one of those free city bikes. Hoped not. She could be miles away by now.

Stay positive, Tyler.

Next to the starting line was Leeds Museum. I don't really do museums but thought it might be the sort of place Spider would go. She liked books, maybe she liked art too, and it was free to get in. There weren't many people inside, but those who were looked like they loved it. I saw a man, hands behind his back, staring at a painting for about a minute. Don't know how long you're meant to look at a painting, but that seemed ridiculous. You look, see a picture of a horse or something, and move on. Maybe the man was homeless, killing time by gawping at old drawings before he got thrown out.

There was no sign of Spider.

I walked out, past some people playing chess on the streets, and finally found Leeds Cathedral. It was about ten times bigger than the last church I'd seen. Decided to go inside.

I'm not really into buildings, apart from my old house in Chiswick, but I have to say this place was pretty amazing. The arched ceiling was so high it hurt my neck to look at it, the windows had more colours than Spider's arm, and everywhere you turned there were statues. After the hustle and bustle of the streets it was nice to be somewhere peaceful, with flickering candles lighting the gloom. It was like a spa dedicated to God.

I saw a sign about Saint Anthony, the patron saint of lost items. Bet on his deathbed that Anthony hoped he might be made a saint of something more important, like peace or prosperity. But they probably already had saints for those. They needed someone to be in charge of Lost Property, so they gave it to him.

This was the prayer you could say to him:

I beseech you most humbly and earnestly to take me under your protection in my present necessities and to obtain for me the favour I desire (State your intention).

I said this little prayer and inserted Spider in the intention bit. She wasn't a missing item, but she was missing. Maybe Saint Anthony would do his stuff and help me find her.

I walked round the cathedral. Up ahead was a group of old people looking at pictures of Jesus dragging his cross. Others were dotted about, sitting on benches. They all seemed smartly dressed, but that didn't mean they weren't homeless. Spider dressed fairly normally, and she didn't have a home. I thought I'd better take a closer look at them, to see if there were any clues.

I spotted a middle-aged man in a coat that looked ready for a charity shop. His hair was sticking up, as if he'd been sleeping badly. He had his head down, hands clamped together tight like he had a butterfly in there. He looked like the bloke on the bus. Could he be homeless? Only one way to find out.

I shuffled down the bench next to him. 'Excuse me,' I whispered.

Don't think he heard me. He'd dived too deep into his thoughts.

'Excuse me,' I said, a bit louder.

He turned to me with an expression that was a quarter curiosity, three-quarters irritation.

'What?' he grunted.

'Are you homeless?'

'I beg your pardon. I own a five-bedroom home in Headingley. Without a mortgage, I'll have you know. Do I look like a homeless person?'

A bit.

'No, I just … I just…' *Just what, Tyler? Just being a complete numbskull.* 'Thought you were someone I knew.'

I shuffled my bum along the bench as fast as I could. The man shook his head and went back to his clenching.

Time to get out of here.

I walked into the daylight, wondering what to do next. Homeless-people spotting isn't easy. There are those lying in doorways and on benches. They're easy to tick off. But there must be plenty of others who don't do that. Ones who walk around looking for somewhere to spend the night, or sitting on benches, or walls, wondering what to do next. They could look like anybody.

All this searching had made me hungry. I found a shop and bought a chicken sandwich, a packet of cheese-and-onion crisps and a big bottle of Coke. Mum hates me drinking Coke. Calls it black sugar. But she wasn't here to stop me. I found a bench and ate my lunch. Having eaten and burped out the last of my Coke I got up and went back to the shop. I felt guilty – all those people outside, with nothing to eat. I bought a cheese and pickle sandwich and soon found someone curled up in a sleeping bag. They had long, grey hair. No idea if it was a man or a woman. I left the sandwich. Hope they liked my choice.

I wandered around, but to be honest there wasn't much method in my wandering. Up one street, back down the other side, peering up alleyways, looking behind hedges. Still no luck.

I tried Spider's phone again and got the same annoying message.

'*The number you are trying is not reachable.*'

I put myself in Spider's trainers. When she was sleeping rough in Ilkley she'd gone to the woods. Maybe that's where she felt safest, away from the crowds and the crazies. I wondered where the biggest woods were round here. A city map told me. Roundhay Park, the biggest bit of green in Leeds. I decided to head there.

After a lot of trudging I made it to the park. It was huge, with lakes and fountains, cafés and gardens. But what I needed was foliage. If Spider was here, she wouldn't be in the open, sunbathing, she'd be on the edges, under a bush or beneath a tree, reading one of her books. I walked and walked and walked, but still no sign of her.

But there was something I hadn't been paying much attention to. The time. I looked at my watch: 7.22 p.m.

Whoa.

I was going to be mega-late. Mum would want to know why I hadn't contacted her. Timeliness is one of her big things. Took my phone out and sent her a text.

Having great time at Jack's. See u later, T x

A nano-second later came her reply.

When?

Text u when I'm leaving

TBH thought you'd be home by now

Sorry

Want Dad to pick you up?

No. Jack's mum will bring me.

Ok x

Phew.

It was nearly September, and the sun had already had enough, slipping away over the horizon. My mission to find Spider had failed. I'd looked in dozens of places, but Leeds had thousands of places. I should have known it would take a lot longer than a day to find her. But then a horrible thought emerged. What if she'd gone to a different city? She'd lied to me about her cousin. Maybe she'd lied to me about Leeds. Could have said the first place that popped into her head. She could be anywhere. The thought fired a shiver through me.

Needed to go home.

I carried on walking, but the surroundings didn't look familiar. Too many fields, not enough buildings. My heart began to pound in my ears. Where on earth was I? I spotted a man walking his dog. I ran up to him.

'Excuse me, is this the way to Leeds?' I said, breaths breaking up my words.

'No, lad. Going in totally wrong direction. This is Bardsey. Leeds is back that way,' he said, pointing in the direction from which I'd come.

'How far is it?'

'Miles.'

'Thanks,' I said, even though there was nothing to be thankful for.

I should have found out where I was on Google Maps. Too late now. I checked my pocket. Four pounds fifty. Nowhere near enough to get a taxi back. I was going to be late, so, so late.

I started to run.

Forty-two

●　●　●　●

I thought my cross-country session with Michele had been the worst ever, but it had just been overtaken by this one. Because while that had hurt like crap, the hurt had come to a halt. This one could go on punishing me for months, especially if Mum and Dad found out where I'd been. On top of that I wasn't dressed for running – jeans, jacket, shoes. Sweat was coming out of every pore, running faster than me. Everything ached, especially my brain, busy trying to make up excuses for getting back so late.

I made it to the city centre. But the streets were different now. The shoppers had gone home to drool over their goodies. They'd been replaced by another younger, noisier crowd, with only one thing on their shopping list – alcohol.

A woman walked towards me, legs swaying like Jenga stacks at the end of a game.

'Which way to the bus station?' I gasped.

'That way, lad,' she said, pointing.

I sprinted off, turned a corner and saw a row of buses. There were loads of letters and numbers on the front of them, but not the ones I wanted. Where was the X84?

I spotted a woman in a driver's uniform and ran over to her.

'Can you tell me when the next bus to Ilkley is?' I panted.

'Six twenty-five.'

'In the morning?'

'Aye. Last bus to Ilkley has long gone.'

'What about the train?'

'No trains tonight, love. Engineering works.'

Her words stabbed me.

This cannot be happening. This cannot be happening. Mum thought I was in Blubberhouses, playing video games with Jack. Instead here I was, stuck in Leeds, on my own. What should I do? Call her to come and get me? She and Dad would go mental. They'd taken my money and my phone last time. What would they do this time? Take all my clothes, burn them, then kill me?

But there was still a chance I could get out of this.

I took out my phone and texted Mum, my thumbs shaking, as if I'd been playing video games all night.

Staying overmight at Jack's x

My heart banged like a bass speaker as I awaited her reply.

Do you mean overnight?

Trust her to spot that.

Yes.

You haven't got an overnight bag.

I'll be fine.

Never had a panic attack before, but I felt one couldn't be far away. Was she speaking to Dad about this? Maybe that was the one thing I had in my favour. Mum wouldn't dare tell him she'd given me my phone.

Wish you'd told me about this.

Yes, but when do sensible and Tyler Jackson ever appear in the same sentence?

Sorry.

Not a word I use very often, but it worked.

See you tomorrow x

I'd done it.

Then reality turned up and kicked me where it hurts.

I was going to have to spend the night on the streets.

Forty-three

I walked aimlessly round. There wasn't a lot else to do. I trudged past endless buildings, now empty, dark, uninviting. I watched as a shopkeeper dragged down steel shutters and padlocked the metal sheet to the ground. Then a man in suit took out some keys and locked the doors to a building. A glowing office block up ahead suddenly turned black as all the lights were snuffed out. It seemed the world was closing down around me.

I stopped underneath a streetlight and took out my wallet again, hoping I'd missed a note, folded up tight. Still four pounds fifty. Not enough for a hotel room, a bed and breakfast, a taxi. Not enough for anything, apart from a bus that wasn't there. The night suddenly felt colder. Up ahead I could see people staggering towards taxis and buses. They'd soon be home, balled tight as hedgehogs under their duvets. And then there was me. No bed, no sheets, no roof. Just the clothes I was standing in.

It made me realise how easy my life was. Twenty steps to the kitchen for as much food or drink as I wanted. Thirty steps to the bathroom for the toilet, a wash or a shower. Forty steps to my bedroom, and a comfy bed, a pillow, a duvet, and a good night's sleep. But out here, nothing was close.

I felt like people were watching me. *Why's that kid just standing there? Shouldn't he be off home? Maybe he's a thief? Or a runaway? Or on drugs? Maybe we should call the police.* I felt scared. I wanted to disappear, to be somewhere safe. I imagined that this is what it's like for Spider, every single night, desperately searching for somewhere she'd come to no harm. No wonder she got panic attacks. Now wonder she got so angry with me for moaning about things that don't really matter.

Up ahead was an alleyway. I stepped into it. The darkness swallowed me whole. I went over to a wall, slid down, knees tight against my chest. Why the hell didn't I check the time of the last bus? Because I'm an idiot, that's why. An idiot to think I could find a girl in a city I didn't even know. I'd felt lonely when I left all my friends behind in London, but the loneliness paled in comparison to this. I never really thought I was afraid of much. But I was afraid of the night to come.

Tiredness was seeping into me. I'd walked miles looking for Spider and run nearly all the way back to the city centre for a bus that wasn't there. The wall behind and the concrete below offered nothing in the way of comfort. I got to my feet, stretched my arms and yawned. I needed to find somewhere to sleep. But where? My mind began racing through places I could go. I'd spotted some benches near the bus station, but it was too bright and too busy. I didn't want police officers or charity people asking me what I was doing or where my mum and dad were. Then there were the shop doorways down Briggate. But I didn't want to take someone else's spot or come across the rough-looking guys I'd seen earlier.

I left the alleyway and walked back the way I'd come. I don't really like crowds, though now that they'd gone, I missed them. The streets were probably no more dangerous than they'd been six hours ago, but logic is never there when you want it. Fear was welling up inside, grabbing hold of me. I felt like a kid again.

All I needed was somewhere quiet to curl up and sleep. Was that too much to ask? I walked slowly up a side street, looking for a suitable spot. Across the road I spotted a doorway. I walked over and looked in. It was about a twentieth of the size of my bedroom, but the place was empty, and the streetlight was broken, painting the doorway black. Not the ideal place to spend seven hours, but I was too tired to find anything better. I lay down in the corner, using my jacket as a pillow, my knees curled up tight.

My eyelids had barely lowered when I heard voices, loud ones. Young guys trying, and failing, to sing.

The voices grew louder.

Glass shattered.

I got to my feet and pressed myself tight against the wall, trying to become the wall. The group was right in front of my doorway. Even in the feeble light I could make out their shapes, at least six of them, pushing, shoving, shouting, swearing. They were all bigger than me. Would they pick on a younger lad? They might. Northern teams hated teams from London. I didn't have my Brentford shirt on, but I had my London voice. That might be all it took.

I hoped they'd soon pass, so I could return to my concrete bed, but as this thought materialised, one of them approached the doorway. Why was he coming in here? Couldn't he see that the shop was shut? I squeezed myself further into the darkness, trying to make myself disappear.

He stepped in, his back to me. I know you can't hear a heartbeat without a stethoscope, but I was sure he could hear mine.

B-bum. B-um. B-um.

The sound of a zip.

The guy groaned. Then I heard what sounded like a tap, on full flow. The tap went on and on. I could feel liquid under my feet.

'Get bloody move on,' came a voice.

'Tha' can't mess with nature,' he said.

Didn't think it was possible to urinate for that long. Mine normally last about twenty seconds. This guy must have a bladder the size of a bath.

The thin layer of liquid became a puddle.

Then a lake.

Finally, he stopped.

Zipper zipped.

'Eeh, that's better,' he sighed.

He lurched out and staggered up the road, following the noise. I didn't need a torch to know that my bedroom was now uninhabitable. I held my nose and waited for the sound to fade to nothing, before grabbing my jacket and stepping out. They were now a long way up the street. But the damage had been done. My jacket was sopping. Of all the shop doorways in Leeds, why the hell did he have to pee in mine? My jacket wasn't just wet, it stank. I wanted to hurl it into the nearest bin, but how would I explain that one away?

Left my jacket at Jack's.

You'd better go and get it, then.

I'd have to buy an identical replacement with the money I didn't have. Which meant I'd have to steal one. The night was getting worse and worse.

I needed to clean the jacket, but where? Judging by the people staggering about, some of the bars were still open. I decided to take a chance and went into the nearest one. I knew I was underage, but I was desperate. Pushed open the pub door. The place was packed with people, all jostling. It was like the streets around Brentford after a match. I squeezed my way through the swaying throng and spotted a sign – *Toilets*.

I found the gents' and hurried in. A couple of guys were peeing at the urinal. I went over to the sink, put my jacket in, covered it in liquid soap and ran the taps.

'Check this out,' said one of them, zipping up his fly.

'There's a laundrette down't road, lad,' said the other, laughing.

Lucky for me, they ignored the sinks and hurried out, keen to get more drink in them. I washed the jacket as best I could and held it under the hand dryer. I'd need to stand there for an hour to dry it. But at least it was clean, and the smell had gone. I was mad thirsty and stuck my head under the tap to glug some water. Felt better after that.

I walked out of the pub, holding my wet jacket away from me, wondering what to do next. I remembered Spider telling me that at night it was safer to keep walking. If I found somewhere to lie down someone might rob me or hit me or stab me. But I'm not as street-hardened as Spider. I'm used to a bedroom and a duvet. I couldn't last another hour, let alone till 6.25 a.m. I had to get some sleep.

I found a narrow lane. There were no lights and it took my eyes time to get used to the darkness. It was the back of a row of shops, with loading bays and a concrete shelf underneath giant steel shutters. Better still, I noticed that someone had left some cardboard out. Street people use it to lie on. The world's thinnest mattress.

I scrambled on to the shelf. The jacket was still way too wet to lie on, so I shoved it in the corner, curled up on the cardboard and closed my eyes. Sleep was as elusive as Spider. The day had been warm, though the heat had all but evaporated. The night was cloudless, a myriad stars above my head, like a giant, glowing join-the-dots.

I was freezing. But that wasn't the only thing making sleep impossible. The ground was rock hard. It would take more than a thin sliver of cardboard to take the edge off that. I so wanted this night to end. It had only just begun.

I turned my face to the shutters, wrapped my arms tight around me, trying, and failing, to stop my incessant shivering. I would never call Ilkley Lido cold again. I closed my eyes, waiting for sleep. But a moment later I felt a sharp prod in my back.

'What the hell you doing here?' came a man's voice.

Forty-four

● ●

I twisted into a piercing light pointing straight at me.
Who was behind it? A policeman? Security guard? Or
someone out to rob me?

'I … I'm just having a lie down.'

'On my cardboard.'

Can you actually own cardboard?

I sat up as the brightness continued to squeeze my
eyes tight.

'You're just a kid.'

Teenager, actually.

The man behind the light turned it on himself. He
had a beard, but he looked young. 'It's okay. Don't be
scared.'

His words calmed me.

Momentarily.

I'd had a lesson in school about Stranger Danger and
knew there were people who preyed on the young. And
that's exactly what I felt like – prey. This guy looked

okay, but I'd watched a programme once about serial killers. They'd all seemed okay too, until their victims ended up in more pieces than a jigsaw puzzle.

'My name's Josh,' he said. 'What's yours?'

Not sure whether I should tell him.

'Jack.'

'What you doing out here, Jack?'

'Looking for a girl, a homeless girl. She's sixteen.'

He sat next to me on the cardboard, not too close, thank goodness. 'Don't get many girls that age on the streets. Way too dangerous.' He turned the light on his phone off. 'Best not draw attention to ourselves.'

'Are you homeless?'

''Fraid so.'

He wasn't how I'd imagined a rough sleeper, well-dressed, well-spoken.

'Why are you looking for this girl?'

I blew out cold air. 'I'm worried about her. She was sofa surfing in Ilkley. Then she told me she was coming to Leeds. But she doesn't know anyone.'

'One of the charity people will find her.'

'So why haven't you been picked up?'

'Guess I'm not vulnerable enough.'

'What do you mean?'

'I'm twenty-four. Male. Not from round here. I don't tick enough boxes.'

'What are you doing on the streets?'

'I don't earn enough for rent and food, so I sleep out here. Until I can get a better job or a cheap flat. Whatever comes first.'

Never knew you could be on the streets and still at work. Didn't make any sense.

'I had a tent,' he went on, 'but someone nicked it. Need to get another one before the weather turns cold.'

'Turns cold? This is freezin'.'

'You're not dressed for it, Jack.'

Understatement of all time.

'Do your parents know you're here?'

'No. They think I'm at a friend's house.'

'This is no place for a kid. I'll take you to the police.'

'No,' I said loudly. 'I'm gonna stay here till six o'clock, then get the first bus back to Ilkley.'

The distant sound of a police siren pierced the night.

'I'll make sure you're okay. Then I'll take you to your bus.'

Forty-five

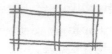

I was still a bit wary of Josh, but my fears were soon washed away.

'You can borrow my sleeping bag if you want.'

I wanted to say no, but it was way too cold to turn down.

'Cheers.'

He unrolled the sleeping bag and I crawled inside. It was a bit pongy, but, unlike cold, I don't think smells have ever killed anyone. Josh put on a couple of extra sweatshirts from his rucksack, pulled his bobble hat down over his head, and settled in a corner of the loading bay.

Despite the sleeping bag the temperature and the concrete conspired against me, making it impossible to snatch any sleep. Instead I lay there, thinking about Spider. For all I knew she might be lying wide awake, just a street away. She'd have a good laugh if she knew I was out here.

Now you knaa what it's like, you little southern softy.

Maybe she'd found a new friend, and was walking the streets, the way she used to. I hoped she was okay.

Then I thought about the thousands of others, lying in doorways and alleys and parks and graveyards, curled up tight, the heat of their bodies deserting them when they needed it most. But I only had to get through a single night. They had endless nights to endure. For some it could even be their last night. No one to help or hold their hand as they slipped away. And in the morning they'd become just another number. One of the four hundred.

I wondered how Josh managed to cope and do a day's work. I struggle to get through school after nine hours in bed. He had to be hard as nails to do this. I hoped he found a new job soon. Or got a pay rise.

I switched channels to think of Mum and Dad back in Fairspew, snuggled under their flowery duvet. Never in a million years could they imagine where I was now, their stroppy son, lying on a piece of discarded cardboard in a stranger's sleeping bag. That sort of thing doesn't happen to the child of Ilkley parents.

At this time of year the nights are short, but this one somehow managed to elongate itself and become the longest ever, the hours too frozen to move. The one thing the homeless have plenty of – time – becomes the most hated thing of all, each second a painful reminder of a hideous existence.

It was a relief when Josh finally elbowed me.

'Better get going, Jack,' he said, stretching his arms.

Wondered who on earth Jack was. Then I remembered it was me.

I looked at my watch: 5.45 a.m.

You have over two hundred bones in your body. Every single one of mine was aching. I needed a full skeleton transplant. Totally knackered. When I got home I'd tell Mum that Jack had snored like a pig and kept me awake all night. Today was officially going to be a duvet day.

Checked my phone. It had died in the night. Probably hypothermia. I put it back in my pocket, grabbed my jacket and crawled off the loading bay. My jacket was still damp. Josh saw me shivering.

'Why not put your jacket on?'

'Someone peed on it.'

If Josh was surprised he didn't show it. Guess that sort of thing happens on the streets.

'Do you want a sweatshirt?'

Another thing to try and explain away.

'No, thanks.'

He shrugged, rolled up his sleeping bag and fastened it to his rucksack. I looked at the loading bay, barely able to believe I'd spent the night there, and thankful I'd never have to again. But Josh had no choice. A piece of cardboard on a slab of concrete – that was his home.

The sun had already appeared, and up ahead I could see the tall buildings of the city. Leeds seemed less scary now. Funny how just a drop of light can do that.

Josh threw his rucksack over his shoulder and we headed towards the bus station.

'Tell me about this girl.'

I told him the full story, between yawns.

'I'll keep my eyes peeled for her. But people on the streets come and go. They're like smoke.'

We walked further into the city. I was glad I'd found Josh. He'd made the night a bit more bearable.

'So what...'

A figure suddenly leaped from a doorway on to Josh's back, sending him sprawling on to the pavement. Josh fell, groaning with the added weight of the man on his back. Then from the shadows stepped another man. He was tall, thin, with lank hair, and eyes devoid of life. He looked like he'd stepped out of a zombie film. But that wasn't all. He held something in his hand. A broken bottle.

Every trace of tiredness fled my body. I stood, eyes wide open, heart hammering, fists clenched.

'No,' I shouted.

But it was going to take more than words to stop this. Josh and the man wrestled on the ground, as zombie man stood over them. 'Ya money,' he screamed.

What money?

Panic had me in its grip. What could I do? Run? But where to? The shops and bars were closed. What were the chances of me finding a policeman at this hour? And if I left Josh it could be all over by the time I got back. For him.

'Leave him alone,' I shouted.

But no one was listening. Josh and the man continued to roll around on the ground, as zombie man stood watching with the jagged bottle, ready to make his move. Just when I thought Josh might be overpowered I saw him raise a fist and deposit it into the face of his assailant. The man yelled and let go of Josh, giving him the chance to get to his feet.

Zombie man stepped forward, waving the bottle madly. Josh slid his backpack off his shoulder and flung it at him, sending the man crashing backwards into a shop front. The bottle smashed on the ground, the weapon splintering into dozens of pieces. The tables had been turned.

Josh picked up the largest piece of broken glass he could find, and held it out, like a knife.

'Clear off,' he screamed.

But they didn't leave without a final flourish. As zombie man hurried past he shoved me as hard as he could. I wasn't expecting it, and went flying, my face hitting the ground hard. I lay, stunned, as the sound of running feet receded.

'Bastards,' shouted Josh, as he hauled me to my feet. 'Are you okay, Jack?'

Don't think I'll ever be okay again. Not after this night.

He turned me over to check my face. I put my hand to my head. It came back red.

'Let me clean you up.'

Josh helped me to a bench. He carefully checked my face for fragments of glass, then took out a bottle of water and a cloth from his rucksack and bathed my cuts. It felt as if he was washing my face in stinging nettles.

'You'll survive,' he said, clearly pleased with his work.

'Who were they?'

'Addicts. They'd eat their own grandmother for drug money.' He looked up the street. 'Poor bastards. But still bastards.'

'Are you okay?'

'Bit shaken. Had a few things happen to me. Nothing as bad as this before.'

Typical that the worst thing happens when I'm here. I thought about Spider. Those guys would have made mincemeat of her. Hoped she was somewhere safe.

'Better get your bus.'

'Yeah.'

We carried on, checking doorways and alleys for anyone who might be out to mug us. But apart from bin collectors and office cleaners we saw no one. In a couple of hours the city would return to normal, workers rushing to their offices with giant tubs of coffee, shoppers, eyes beaming, desperate for more stuff. A world away from the cardboard and the sleeping bags and the cold and the drunks and the drugs and the broken bottles. Leeds had a split personality. Maybe every city does.

We reached the bus station and there was the X84. Never been so pleased to see a bus in my life.

'Guess this is where we say goodbye,' said Josh.

I don't really do guy hugs, but this was an exception. He had after all saved my life.

'Thanks, Josh. Hope everything works out for you.'

'Same for you, Jack. And Spider.'

He shook my hand and turned to leave. I watched him walk away, wondering if he'd turn his life around. I hoped so.

I climbed aboard the bus, went upstairs and found a seat at the back.

Within seconds I was asleep.

Forty-six

I woke as we pulled into Otley.

Today there was no one on the bus who looked even vaguely homeless, just half a dozen sleepy-looking people, going off to work somewhere. As we headed towards Ilkley my thoughts turned to home. Mum would want to know why I'd come back at such an hour. I'd say Jack's mum started work early and needed to drop me off. She'd want to know why I had cuts and bruises on my face. I'd say that we went climbing, and I fell out of a tree. And she'd want to know why my jacket was wet. I'd say we had a water fight.

All bases covered.

But the last thing I needed was an interrogation. I'd say that Jack and I had stayed up stupidly late playing video games, and after listening to his pig snores for the rest of the night I needed to go to bed. She'd rather that than have me lounging around the house all day, moaning my head off.

Ilkley finally appeared. After what I'd been through it actually felt good to be back.

The bus parked at the station and I walked through the town. For the first time since yesterday I felt safe. I turned into my street, but the instant I did I knew something wasn't right. Dad's car was still in the drive. It was 7.40 a.m. Dad always leaves at 7 a.m. sharp. And by always, I mean always. Maybe he was ill or had taken a day's holiday. Whatever the reason, it was a long way from normal.

I walked up the path and got my key out. *Just stay nice and calm. Stick to your story and you'll be fine.* I opened the front door. They were both standing there. The second I saw their faces I knew they knew. Mum had one of those expressions where she couldn't decide whether to hug me or hit me. Dad just looked ferocious.

Mum ran up and held me so tight I thought she was trying to kill me. Then she let go and stared at me, tears filling her eyes. 'Tyler, where have you been?'

'Jack's,' I said, clinging to my lie like wreckage in the sea.

'Don't lie to us,' shouted Dad. 'We know you weren't there last night. Where the hell were you?'

They'd found out. Somehow. It didn't matter how. They knew.

'I went to Leeds,' I said softly.

They both continued to glare at me.

'What are those marks on your face?'

I got pushed to the ground by druggies, who were attacking my friend with a broken bottle.

'I fell over.'

'I'll call the police,' said Mum.

'The police?'

'Yes, the police. Last night I got Jack's mum's number from the class rep. I wanted to thank her for letting you stay. She told me you haven't been to Jack's for months. So then I found Michele's mum's number. Apparently, you'd told Michele you were going to Jack's as well. We had absolutely no idea where you were.'

Oh, holy God.

'In there,' growled Dad, pointing to the sitting room.

Mum took out her phone to call the police as I walked slowly into the sitting room, steeling myself for another interrogation. I dropped my damp jacket on the floor and collapsed on to the sofa. I just wanted to close my eyes, go to sleep and escape to my dreams. But I knew that was impossible. They'd want to know everything.

Mum's mumbled words made their way through the wall. I couldn't hear them clearly, but I knew what they'd be.

Yes, he's back home, officer. Seems to be fine. Spent the night in Leeds. We don't know why yet, but don't worry, we will and we'll let you know. Thanks for all your help.

A moment later the door handle turned and Mum and Dad were standing in front of me, arms folded, matching expressions of fury, just like the day we got back from Wales.

'Tell us what happened,' said Dad, through gritted teeth.

Here we go.

'I went to find Spider, the homeless girl.'

'Oh, you bloody idiot,' he said, slapping his hand hard against the wall. 'How many times do we have to tell you to stay away from people like that?'

'People like what?' I shouted, surprising both myself and them with the volume. 'She's a human being, like us.'

'It's not for you to get involved.'

'But who is getting involved? Not you. You two couldn't care less.'

'Tyler,' shouted Dad.

'It's true. All you're bothered about are kitchens and golf.'

'That is so unfair,' moaned Mum. 'If I didn't care about people, I wouldn't put up with all the hate and misogyny and homophobia and racism I have to watch every single day.'

'And I give to Cancer Research.'

Tick. Tock.

I knew Mum and Dad were mad with me, but they

didn't have a monopoly on madness. I could be mad too.

'Yeah, maybe I should have told you, but if I had you'd have stopped me. Then who would have helped her? And don't say the experts, please don't say the experts.'

The room fell silent as my words went to work on them.

Tick. Tock.

I suddenly realised someone was missing.

'Where's Tallulah?'

'Gone to stay with the Drivers,' said Mum. 'She wondered where you'd gone. I told her you were on a sleepover.'

Guess they didn't want to scare her if they didn't have to.

'We had no idea what had happened to you. I thought you might have met someone online. Someone...'

Mum buried her face in her hands and began to cry.

'I'm sorry, Mum.'

And this time I meant it. They must have been as terrified as me last night. Probably had no sleep. Exhausted. Sick with fear.

Tick. Tock.

But then from nowhere came a solution, a good one, like when the answer in maths appears, when you're convinced there is no answer.

'I was gonna tell you but my phone died.'

Dad stared at me. 'But we took your phone.' Then he stared at Mum. 'You didn't give it back to him, did you?'

Now there were two guilty people in the room. Mum wiped her eyes and fiddled with her wedding ring. 'He said he was going to Jack's and might need it.'

'What would he need it for? It was part of his punishment. We agreed.'

'I know we agreed, Clive, but you weren't there when the issue arose.'

'So you took it upon yourself to give it back?'

'Yes, that's exactly what I did.'

'If he had his phone, why didn't you call him?'

'I did. It went to voicemail.'

'You should have told the police. They can trace phones.'

'Well, I'm sorry, but I was a bit stressed last night, in case you hadn't noticed.'

It was a relief to be out of the firing line, even for a moment. But it didn't take long for them to turn their guns back on me.

'Give me that phone. Now,' shouted Dad.

I decided not to throw it, like last time. Handed it over, and Dad shoved it in his pocket.

'Why didn't you come back?' said Mum.

'Missed my last bus home.'

'You should have gone to the police.'

'Thought you'd go mad.'

'Right there,' said Dad, staring at the lock-up garages over the road. 'All over this bloody girl.'

'This sixteen-year-old girl, Dad. Sixteen, living on the streets. Have you any idea what's that like?'

'No, and I have absolutely no intention.'

'Well, think of the scariest thing that's ever happened to you, then add a bit more scare. Think of the coldest you've ever been, then turn the thermostat down. Think of the most uncomfortable you've been, then add a bit more discomfort. That's what it's like. Night after night after night after night.'

'She is not my responsibility.'

'So whose responsibility is she?'

'We just want you to be safe,' said Mum, tears again pooling in her eyes. 'That's why we're so mad. We had no idea where you'd gone or what had happened. Think about that for a moment.'

I had sympathy for them. If Dexter went missing I'd be chewing the curtains with worry. But I hadn't intended this to happen. If Mum hadn't rung Jack's mum and Michele's mum, everything would have been okay. But things never seem to turn out the way I want.

Tick. Tock.

'I'm sorry.'

'Sorry's not enough,' said Mum.

'You lied to us, Tyler, big time. For the second time. You're not going anywhere for the rest of the holiday,' bellowed Dad, obviously not caring what Vicky next door or the rest of Ilkley might think. 'You're staying in this house and not stepping a foot outside.'

Forty-seven

• •

Convicted.

Two judges. No jury. No court of appeal.

Imprisoned for five whole days. Suppose I couldn't expect anything less. I'd lied to Mum and therefore Dad. I'd gone looking for the girl they didn't want me to look for. I'd scared the pants off them.

I trudged upstairs to my room, lay on the bed, and fell fast asleep. My sleep was surprisingly dream-free, my brain too tired to make anything up. I woke mid-afternoon to find it working overtime. Yesterday came rushing back like a spring tide, all of the horrible events queuing to get inside. And once in, I couldn't get them out. But one was bigger than all the others. In spite of everything I'd done, I didn't deserve my punishment. I wanted to stop arguing with Mum and Dad, but how could I when they did something like this? Where was the justice? Had I really done something that wrong?

A row. Wondered if that's how Spider's troubles

had started. Something small that grew, brick by brick, until it became a wall between Spider and her family, an obstacle too high to climb, too solid to break through. And then she was on her own. No going back. There was now a wall between me and my parents. They'd put up half the bricks. I'd built the rest. But unlike Spider's wall, I guess one day we'd smash it down. And things would go back to something like normal. But what about her?

I climbed off my bed and glanced out of the window. Dad's car had gone. He'd be at work now, seething. I'd hate to be the next golf ball he hit. I could hear Mum slamming cupboard doors, not caring if they fell off, and Dexter emitting the odd bark, not sure what was going on. I couldn't even take Dex for a walk. Life was an almighty lettuce sandwich.

I went back to bed and closed my eyes, but my brain kept playing the box-set that was yesterday. A bit later I heard a familiar voice. The Drivers had brought Tallulah home. I didn't have to wait long to see my sister. The bedroom door burst open and she dived on top of me.

'Oh, Tyler,' she said, hugging me with her skinny arms. 'I've missed you.'

I kissed her head. 'And I've missed you too.'

She lay next to me on the bed, still wearing her outdoor shoes. Shoes on the bed seemed the tiniest of indiscretions after what I'd done.

'You stink,' she exclaimed, pinching her nose. I hadn't summoned up the energy to shower yet. 'Where did you go?'

'To Leeds to look for the homeless girl.'

'Did you find her?'

'No.'

'That was a waste of time, then.' She pulled back to get me into focus. 'What happened to your face?'

'A lion attacked me.'

She smiled. 'Are Mummy and Daddy happy you're home?'

'Wouldn't go that far. They're pretty cross with me. I scared them.'

'Can we go to the park?'

'Love to, but I'm banned from going out.'

'For ever?'

'Till I go back to school. I'm going to lie here for five solid days.'

'Lucky you.' She hugged me again. 'I'm glad you're home.'

And with that, Tallulah leaped off the bed and ran downstairs to carry on with her worry-free seven-year-old existence. Maybe life was once like this for Spider – a mum who loved her, a brother she adored, a group of friends to play with. Not a care in the world. Maybe her life crumbled so slowly she wasn't prepared when it finally fell apart. Or maybe there was one cataclysmic disaster, like the death of her mum, that meant the start of her horror story.

I wished I knew more about her.

But she wasn't the only person in my life I had to think about. There was Michele. She'd have heard from her mum that I'd gone missing. Then she'd have heard I was no longer missing. She'd wonder why I'd lied to her again. Why I hadn't called her. My phone would be filled with messages.

Ty, where did you go? xx

Ty, why haven't you called me? x

Ty, I'm waiting.

I could ignore Michele for a while, but I couldn't ignore her for ever. I needed to do something about her. But what? She'd be furious about where I'd gone, and who I'd gone to look for. Maybe I wouldn't have to do anything at all. Maybe she'd dump me by text, like she did with Luke. For once I was glad I didn't have my phone, waiting for the ping that says, *Goodbye and good riddance, Ty. Blah, blah, blah.*

But Michele is nothing if not unpredictable.

An hour later my bedroom opened to reveal Mum, arms folded, still refusing to let go of her angry face. 'Michele's at the front door, asking after you. What do you want me to do?'

I stared up at the ceiling. Could have lied again and said I was sick, but that was only delaying the inevitable.

'Send her up.'

Within seconds my bedroom door flew open and there stood Michele. But instead of a scowl, she wore a huge grin.

'Ty,' she cried, diving on top and wrapping her arms around me. A second after the wrapping, she unwrapped herself, backed off and started sniffing.

'I haven't had a shower yet.'

'It's nearly half-five. Are you sick?'

'Tired, that's all.'

She leaned back to look at my face. 'What happened? I want to know everything.'

It was time to call a halt to the lies.

'Michele, I didn't go to Jack's. I went to Leeds to look for Spider. I walked for miles and miles but couldn't find her. I missed my last bus back and spent the night on the streets. I got pushed over by a druggy who looked like a zombie. Mum and Dad have barred me from going out.'

Michele stared at me, eyes popping, her brain having gorged on too much information, unable to swallow, let alone digest. For once she seemed lost for words. But the words she finally came up with were the last ones I was expecting.

'I forgive you, Ty.'

Maybe the cold had damaged my hearing.

'What?'

'I know you feel something towards that stupid, hopeless case. You can't help that. But she's gone now. You need to forget her.'

Michele never ceased to amaze me. I thought she'd go pitbull-crazy and add to my bruises. But, no, she was prepared to forgive me.

'You're not angry?'

''Course I'm angry, you turnip. You did something unbelievably stupid, looking for that skinny waste of space. But it's just us now,' said Michele, shuffling closer to me, and putting her hand on mine.

I needed to call time-out.

'I've got to have a shower.'

Michele pinched her nostrils with her fingers and spoke like an alien. 'That's the most sensible thing you've ever said.'

I grabbed some clean clothes and padded down the corridor to the bathroom, making sure I locked the door. Wouldn't put it past Michele to try and get in. I stripped off, and let the water do its stuff. As I stood there in the warm cascade, I wondered what to do next. Michele was both gorgeous and jarring. Was I just being seduced by that body and that tan? The tan would be gone by October, and while her body would still be there it would be mostly covered by school uniform. Was she right for me? Was she good for me?

It was decision time.

Having dried and dressed I went back to my room
to a sight that would keep me awake at nights. Michele
had taken her hoody off, to reveal a low-cut T-shirt
revealing far more than it hid. She was lying, stretched
out on my bed, arms behind her head, a mischievous
smile on her face.

'Looking much better, Mr Jackson.'

Michele never made things easy for me. I needed to
do this quickly. Decided to borrow another line from
one of Mum's TV dramas. 'Michele, I don't think this
is working.'

'What do you mean?' she said, her face crumpling.

'I mean, I don't think we should go out.' Just in case
that's what we were doing.

'But we were getting on so well.'

Perhaps in Michele's mind.

'Yes, but I'm not...' What was I not? Man enough?
Boy enough? Brave enough? Stupid enough? 'Not ready
enough.'

'It's that Spider girl, isn't it?'

'No.' Although in a funny sort of way it was. Spider
had taught me something new – pride. Could I possibly
have any self-respect going out with a girl who acted the
way Michele did, who said the things she said?

Michele looked crushed. 'I need you, Ty.'

Maybe that's what it was all about. For whatever
reason Michele needed to have a boy in her life.

'I'm sorry.'

I wanted to hug her, but I knew that in the current situation, Michele wearing very little, lying on my bed, it could be a very dangerous move indeed.

'You have made a big mistake.'

And with that she grabbed her hoody, leaped off my bed and ran out of the room.

Forty-eight

● ●

● ● ●

The five days passed like slow-moving traffic. With no pool to go to, no Spider to teach, no Michele to argue with, no Dexter to walk, no TV to watch, I was too bored to even yawn. I occasionally put my hand to my heart just to check that my life hadn't actually ground to a halt.

It was almost a relief when school started. It was good to see some familiar faces. What wasn't so good was what came out of these faces – exciting stories of holidays in far-flung places. My zip wire in Wales didn't really stack up.

It also gave me a chance to catch up with my two flaky friends, Dom and Jack. Dom looked like he'd been dipped in the same pot as Michele, having spent seven weeks in the south of France, and Jack, although lacking in tan, was not lacking in stories, having been on an action-packed adventure holiday in the Alps. I'd wait and see how things went, but I wasn't going to go running after them like an over-excited puppy.

And then there was Michele.

She gave me the full works – the evil eye, the scowl, the nose in the air, the cold shoulder. I knew I'd done the right thing. This was reinforced a few weeks later when I saw her with Toby Yorke, a lad from my class, running up Wells Road. Toby looked as if he was in need of an ambulance. Her running ruse seemed like the first thing she did with prospective boyfriends, to see if they had what it takes to go out with her. Toby failed the test miserably. Apparently he only made it as far as the moor and threw up in Ilkley Tarn.

So why did Michele choose me? Seeing as it was summer, maybe the pool of available boys was quite thin. Or she had a thing for London boys. Whatever the reason it was time to move on, as Mum would say. I even decided to delete the photo of her in the red swimsuit.

I found it.

My god, that bikini suits her.

I pressed the dustbin symbol.

'Goodbye, Michele.'

And just like that she was gone.

But there were two people who wouldn't be going anywhere.

My parents.

Things continued to be bitterly cold at home, though as the weeks passed words began to flow, even some nice ones, like 'morning', 'hello', and 'sleep well?' But it wasn't until October that the Ice Age finally came to an end. I'd been upstairs doing my homework when Mum shouted for me to come down. I closed my laptop, clomped downstairs and looked in the dining room. It was set for a family dinner. Four of us. I was being invited back into the fold. Unless, of course, they were about to evict me, and the place was set for our new lodger.

I trudged into the sitting room, to find Mum and Dad on the sofa, half-smiles on their faces. They were close together, holding hands, like on that fateful day in London.

'Sit down, love,' said Mum.

Love? Really must check my hearing.

I sat opposite them.

Tick. Tock.

'How's school?'

Shrug.

'And Michele?'

'Not seeing her any more.'

'I didn't know that.'

'You do now.'

'Are you upset?'

'No.'

Maybe that's what they'd got me down for – The Tyler News. And now that it was over: the weather.

Tick. Tock.

'We've been talking about what happened,' said Dad. 'And we want to apologise.'

If my bum hadn't been parked so far back I'd have fallen off the chair.

'Apologise?'

'Yes,' said Mum. 'We overreacted a bit. But you must understand, we weren't just angry, we were scared.'

'Of what?'

'Losing you.'

'I only went to Leeds.'

'You'll understand,' said Mum. 'One day. When you have kids.'

Please god, tell me this isn't a sex education talk.

'We want to talk about Spider.'

Seriously?

They looked at me, then the furniture, as if not quite sure what to say next.

'She meant a lot to you, didn't she?' said Mum softly.

'Yeah. Not at first, but by the end, yeah. She meant a lot. Means a lot.'

I started to feel a bit emotional. Never had a conversation like this before.

Tick. Tock.

'I'd like to have met her.'

'Yeah, she was funny. Dead funny.'

'I shouldn't have said what I said,' went Dad.

Had Mum been having a go at him or had he come up

with this himself? My money was on Mum. But they'd both changed lately. She'd stopped her job watching awful stuff online and started work at a garden centre. And Dad had begun getting home a bit earlier. Maybe he'd got faster at his job, or was driving back quicker. Whatever the reason, he wasn't as spiky as he'd once been. They both seemed more relaxed.

'We've been reading about the homeless situation.'

Reading it. They should try doing it.

Tick. Tock.

'It's very sad.'

'Being sad isn't enough.'

But then Dad said something I never thought I'd hear.

'That's why we'd like to help.'

Forty-nine

●

Woman's body found in *River Aire*.

My stomach lurched as I read the online news. A corpse had been seen by a couple walking over Leeds Bridge. The body of a young woman was later retrieved from the water by police. Investigations still ongoing as to her identity.

I closed the laptop.

Could it be Spider? Possibly. I'd taught her to swim, sort of, and she was used to cold water. But what if the river had been fast-flowing, and it was dark, and she was fully clothed? No one could survive that. The fear lasted a full day, until I learned that the victim had been a student, who, after a night of binge drinking, had got separated from her friends and fallen in the river. Awful way to go. But the incident made me realise what danger Spider was in. As part of their peace-offering Mum and Dad had given me back my phone, and I'd tried to call her on many occasions, but each time got the same annoying message. To make matters worse, we still hadn't heard anything from the local council or the charity people. They'd told me there were lots of outreach workers on the street. So why hadn't they reached out and found her? Maybe Spider had found an amazing place to hide, or perhaps she'd left Leeds. Or maybe she'd never gone to Leeds in the first place. But I had a feeling she was still there.

I wanted to try one more thing to find her, and I still had the offer of help from Dad sitting on the table, unopened. I couldn't quite believe he'd agreed to help. Maybe the stories he'd read had changed his mind. Perhaps for the first time he realised that the safety net doesn't always work. There are those who fall through, with no one to catch them.

My idea to find Spider came when Tallulah was clearing out her old toy cupboard. She had a full-on addiction to soft toys and although she was also into smartphones and tablets, it didn't quench her love for all things soft and furry, especially if they were on the verge of being thrown out.

You can't throw that out. I love it.

She'd made two piles, a tiny one, with stuff for the charity shop, and a gigantic one with the toys she couldn't bear to part with, even though she hadn't so much as looked at them in three years. It was in the tiny reject pile that I saw them, and my idea was born.

'Dad, you know you said you'd like to help Spider?'

'Yes,' said Dad, with the enthusiasm of someone beginning to regret that statement.

'Can we go to Leeds on Sunday? I've had an idea.'

'What idea?'

'I'll tell you when we get there.'

I was worried that if I told Dad my idea now it wouldn't get a metre off the launchpad. But if I told him in Leeds, it would be too late for him to back out.

'Hope this isn't going to be a wild goose chase.'

'The wildest,' I said, smiling.

And so, on Sunday, he drove us in. He even let me listen to Radio 1. It was like having a different Dad next to me. I liked it.

He parked opposite Trinity Leeds, climbed out and stood, arms folded, a fake angry look on his face. 'Okay, Tyler Jackson, you've dragged me into Leeds city centre when I could be on the first tee at Ilkley Golf Club. Are you finally going to tell me what this is all about?'

I pulled a handful of Tallulah's coloured chalks from my pocket.

'Chalk?'

'Yeah, we're gonna write messages.'

'Messages? Are you mad?'

'Maybe. I reckon Spider is hiding somewhere no one can find her, but sooner or later she'll walk the streets. We'll leave a message for her.'

'What sort of message?'

'*Spider, get in touch, T.* Something like that.'

'We could get arrested.'

'It's chalk, Dad, not paint. It'll rub off in a few days.'

'But what if someone sees me?'

'Chill out, it's Sunday. And if someone asks what you're doing, tell them.'

Although I sensed he hated the idea, he couldn't think of a single good reason not to give it a go. On top of that he'd offered to help.

'Okay, let's get this madness over with,' he sighed.

I gave him some of the coloured chalk.

'You do the city centre west of Briggate, I'll do the east. We'll meet back at the car in an hour.'

'You really have thought this through, haven't you?'

'Yep.'

And so Dad and I set off on our lightweight graffiti campaign. Most of the shops hadn't opened yet and the streets were quiet. But the world of the homeless never closes. I saw sleeping bags and bodies scrunched in doorways, bus shelters and under awnings. I looked for the black sleeping bag, green rucksack, blue hoody, white trainers, that tattooed arm. But, no, Spider remained as elusive as the wind.

I started as far east as I planned to go, the coach station. Kneeling on the pavement I wrote my first message: *Spider, hope you're ok. Contact me, T.* Decided not put my full name. Didn't want anyone to trace it. I then worked my way north to Eastgate, down towards Kirkgate Market, past the Corn Exchange, up one side of Briggate and down the other. I got a few funny looks from early-bird shoppers and people on their way to work, but nobody seemed that bothered. You get plenty of weirdos in Leeds.

By the time I'd been past the Arcades and reached the bottom of the pedestrian section I reckon I'd written about twenty-five messages. If Dad had done the same, that was fifty in all. Unless Spider decided to keep her chin up and admire the rooftops, there was a good chance she'd spot at least one of them.

I got back to the car park to find a very flustered-looking Dad.

'What's up?'

'I got chased down the street by a café owner saying I was bad for trade.' I laughed. 'It's not funny.' Dad breathed out heavily. 'Okay, it is a bit funny.'

'I'm proud of you, Dad.'

'Good. Now let's go home.'

Fifty

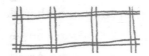

The day after the chalking the rain came. By the bucketload.

'Did you write any of your messages under cover?'

'A few,' said Dad.

It was as though God had decided to ruin my plan by unzipping a few clouds over Leeds. Probably only ten per cent of them would have survived. Five messages. Was it enough? It would have to be. A tug of war couldn't drag Dad back to write new ones, and they wouldn't let me go on my own. I'd done all I could to find Spider. I'd run out of ideas. And I'd used up my Dad-favour. There was nothing more to do.

Life trundled along as normal for the next week. I went to school. I kept out of elbowing distance of Michele. I walked Dexter. And talked to Dexter.

'What we gonna do now, Dex?'

Dexter always looked keen to answer but never put his keenness into anything other than panting.

'If only Spider could turn herself into a stick, you'd bring her back.'

Dexter's tongue lolled out.

'Just you and me – again.'

It wasn't a bad existence, but nor was it the one I wanted. Apart from my family I'd had four people in my life. Now I had two flaky friends and a dog. Guess I was just going to have to get used to it.

Four o'clock, Monday afternoon. The worst day of the week was nearly over. I walked out of school on to Cowpasture Lane, a name that couldn't be more countrified if it tried. I had biology homework, which never failed to impact on my body. Today it was making me walk incredibly slowly towards home, and my desk.

I strolled down the high street past The Black Hat.

'Dead canny swimmer, yous.'

I turned, and there, standing in a doorway grinning, was the girl I'd been looking for. Spider stepped out and hugged me so hard you'd think I was family. I hugged her back, not caring who saw.

We finally let go.

I stood back. She looked so different. The last time I'd seen her she had lank hair, lifeless eyes, a face devoid of any discernible colour, a spider on its last legs. But she'd metamorphosed. Her hair was short and shiny. Her eyes now came with added sparkle. Her cheeks were red, but then she had just hugged a schoolboy in the high street. She even seemed to have put on weight.

'What happened?' I said, scarcely able to believe who I was talking to.

'Let's gan to the park, and I'll tell yous.'

We walked down Lister Street to the Riverside Gardens, found a bench in the park and sat down. The smiles hadn't once left our faces.

'So?' I said.

'So what?'

'What the heck happened?'

Spider put her hands on her thighs. I noticed her jeans now came without ventilation holes.

'Was a bloody nightmare to start with. Got to Leeds. Didn't have a clue what to do or where to gan.'

'Why did you tell me you had a cousin there?'

Spider looked over at two boys using trees for goal posts. 'Felt ashamed. Wanted yous to think I could sort myself out.'

'Why?'

'Pride, I guess.'

That word again.

'And you'd already done more than enough.'

'But you needed help.'

'Did I ever. Wandered aboot a bit. Nearly got jumped a few times. Someone nicked me phone.' Explained the stupid message I kept getting. 'Effing scary, man.

Couldn't sleep. Dead cold. Dead everything. Nearly came back to those bastard woods,' said Spider, looking in the direction of Middleton. 'But then I had me first ever bit of luck. Apart from meeting yous.'

Grin.

'I was clammin. That's hungry for you non-Geordie speakers,' said Spider, reading the confusion on my face. 'Couldn't wait for the soup wagons. Was that desperate I went in a Middle Eastern café and asked this gadgie if he had any spare food. Thought he might throw me through his shop window, but instead he asked what had happened. Told him. Everything.' Spider pressed pause on her story as she blinked away tears. 'He said … he said he'd give me more than food, he'd give me a job, and a room.'

And then the tears came, great big ones that no amount of blinking could stop. I put a hand on Spider's arm. She took my hand and held it tight.

'Sorry, Tyler, man. Thought you were a one-off, that nobody out there gave a bloody monkey's. But I met someone else who did. How lucky am I?'

Luck had been in such short supply for Spider, but she'd finally got some. It wasn't some fluky goal sort of luck, it was far better than that. It was the luck to find a decent man who was prepared to give something and expect nothing back. Couldn't have been happier for her.

'Even let me stay rent-free, till I got some money.'

'Straight up?'

'Vertical. And it wasn't a sofa neither. It was a sofa bed. Get me, a sofa-bed surfer.'

We both smiled.

'But was dead worried he'd want something more from me, other than serving and wiping tabletops. But he didn't. Instead he told me his story. He was from Syria. Lost his mam and sister to the bombing in Homs. Managed to make it to the UK and start again. Said he'd been given a second chance, and if the opportunity ever came he'd give someone else another chance. I was that person. Tyler, it was like I'd won the bloody lottery.'

Now it was my turn to blink tears away. But this time they were happy ones. Of all the people in the country it had taken a foreigner to give her the safety and security she needed. We hugged each other again. If what I'd just heard didn't deserve a hug nothing does.

'Did the charity people not find you?'

'Aye, couple of guys tried to persuade me to seek Children's Services. But I was too stubborn. Mind, if I'd had to spend another week on those streets, I'd have gone with them.'

'I came looking for you.'

'Why?'

'Met your cousin again. Found out you were sixteen.'

'Never said I wasn't.'

'Thought you were older, what with your tattoo and everything.'

Spider looked down at the swirls on her arms. 'You can get owt when you're on the streets.'

Decided not to tell her about my night in Leeds. Probably pathetic in comparison with what she'd had to put up with. And didn't want to tell her about the problems it had caused. That was my fault, not hers.

'Met a guy called Josh. Do you know him?'

Spider shook her head. 'Met a ton of people on the street. Some good. Some bad. Just people, really.'

'Anyway, couldn't find you. But you found me.'

'Aye, saw one of your messages at a bus stop.' Wait till I tell Dad his Sunday wasn't wasted. 'Don't know many Ts in Yorkshire. Was trying hard to forget you, Tyler.'

'Why?'

She rubbed her hand over her mam tattoo.

'It's difficult, man. Had some good memories here, some bad ones too. And that row we had in the woods. Me mam said never gan to sleep on an argument. Though they managed to never gan to sleep without one.' She blew out air. 'I wanted to see yous again. I missed you.'

'Me?'

'No, that spotty kid over there on the slide. Yes, you.'

The thought warmed me from the inside out.

'I was lonely here, dead lonely. Just wandering around. Nothing to do. Didn't know anyone other than Chrissie and her bastard boyfriend. You were my only friend.' She took my hand and held it tight. 'I wanted to say sorry.'

'What for?'

'For not telling yous about me and what was really gannin on. For not paying you enough. For being an idiot with the wet towel and the key and losing the money you earned.'

Her hand disappeared into her pocket and pulled out some notes. Although I'd been angry with Spider for losing my money, time had eroded the anger to nothing.

'Keep it.'

'Divvent want to keep it. Want you to have it,' she said, thrusting the money at me.

'You earned it.'

'No, Tyler. Take it, please.'

Sometimes it's better to take than to give.

'Thanks.'

I took the money and put it in my blazer pocket.

'I've also got something else for you.' She opened up her bag and pulled out four books. I'd forgotten all about them. 'Want you to have these too. Don't want to be someone who just takes.'

'Mum didn't even notice they'd gone.'

'Doesn't matter. They're yours. Not mine.'

Took the novels and put them in my backpack. I'd find a time to slip them into our mini library. I'd got back into Mum and Dad's good books. Didn't want to be thrown out of them again.

'So what about yous? How're your mam and dad?'

'Pretty happy. They've got their new kitchen.'

'Divvent care aboot that, man. I mean between you and them?'

'Life's better. Much better. We don't always agree, but we don't argue either, not like we used to. The war with Mum and Dad is finally over.'

'Happy for yous.'

'I'd like you to meet them.'

'Aye, maybe one day.'

Spider went quiet for a bit, probably thinking about her own family. I hoped they'd take her back. If only so she could see her brother. The swimmer.

'What about that lass who was after you?'

'She's gone. Kaput.'

'You did right there. She's a wrong'un.'

'Don't think she's wrong. She's got some issues to resolve.'

'Haven't we all?'

Spider seemed calmer, more content. It's amazing what having your own bed can do for you.

'We should go for a swim sometime.'

'Aye, I'd like that. I'd like that a lot.'

I looked over in the direction of the town. 'You gonna see your cousin?'

Spider followed my look. 'Na, she's had her chance. Could have stood up to that boyfriend of hers. Could have helped me but didn't. Chrissie is history.'

'What you gonna do now?'

'You know those boulders way up there?' she said, looking at the Cow and Calf Rocks, high on the moor.

Nodded.

'Promised myself I'd gan up there one day. Today is that day. Come if you like.'

Much as I wanted to spend more time with Spider, I also knew I had to get home.

'Another day.'

'Fair enough. Gonna be a canny long time up there.' Spider smiled. Her hand disappeared into her pocket again and she gave me a card with a name on the front: *Jamal's.* 'There's a free kebab in Leeds waiting for you.'

'I'll take you up on that,' I said, salivating at the prospect of all that meat on a stick.

It was so good to see Spider again. And what was even better was seeing her happy. She was safe, had a job, and a bed. Three things that had seemed impossible all those weeks ago.

'I'd better be off,' I said. 'Mum'll be wondering where I am.'

'Never want to upset your mam.'

I got her phone number, and we shared another gigantic hug. And then she did something I wasn't expecting. She gave me a quick kiss on the lips. It wasn't a Michele sort of kiss. It was a thanks-for-all-you've-done one.

But it still felt good.

Out of the corner of my eye I saw some kids from my class looking over at us. The rumour factory was open for business.

I turned to them. 'This is my friend, Spider,' I shouted. 'And she's brilliant.'

They looked away. This time it was them that were embarrassed, not me.

'Take care of yersel, bonny lad.'

'You too.'

I headed home.

Spider turned towards the moor.

Fifty-one

I closed the front door and led Dexter up the street, past the lock-up garages.

'Well, that was a summer and a half, wasn't it, Dex?'

Maybe not for him. But it was for me. I'd thought it would be the most forgettable summer ever, but it turned into the most memorable. And one person had been at the heart of everything – Spider. I sometimes think about what went on, but the thinking doesn't last too long. You can't live your life looking backwards. Mum's got a quote on the kitchen wall: *The past is just the recipe. Today is the cake.*

As Dexter and I walked past the Drivers' house I saw Gatwick staring out of the window, the way cats do, probably thinking, *That's the kid who let that weird girl sleep on our sofa, my sofa. Don't ever let him back in the house again.*

I did the wrong thing, letting Spider stay there. What I should have done was get her to stay at our house. It wouldn't have been easy, but I think I could have done it. That would have shown Mum, and especially Dad, that homeless doesn't equal hopeless, that everyone is the same. They'd have seen that Spider was the victim of bad luck and needed our help. They'd have seen her for what she was – a funny girl, whose life had taken a terrible turn.

Dexter and I carried on through the town and reached the Toy Museum, where Michele had tried to kill me.

'Hills are to be walked up, isn't that right, Dex?'

Not sure he agreed with me, but his tail wagged all the same.

It was a beautiful autumn day, the sun's thermostat set at the ideal temperature, the sky a perfect blue. We walked past the tarn and up the steep paths towards the rocks. I said hello to the walkers I passed along the way. It's the sort of thing you do in these parts. We crossed the little wooden bridge over the boulder-strewn stream and up through the trees. Dexter and I were both panting. Not far to go now.

There was a reason I'd chosen to come here, apart from Dexter and the weather. It was something Spider had said: *Gonna be a canny long time up there.* I think I knew why she'd said this.

We walked over the brow of a hill and there were the Cow and Calf Rocks, deposited by a glacier, or avalanche, or volcano. *Note to self: try to pay more attention in geography.* I used the climb holes and clambered to the top. The views were amazing. Down below, the stone buildings of Ilkley town filled the bottom of the Wharfe Valley. Further afield I could see Middleton Woods, the trees, having got bored with green, now a mix of yellow and orange and red. And in front of the woods a white building, behind which lay Ilkley Lido and Pool. Now that's what I call a fair view. I took as big a breath as my chest could manage. Not a bad place to be, really. Not a bad place at all.

I dug out my phone and found the pictures of my old house in Chiswick. The bedroom. The sitting room. The dining room. The hall. The toilet. The memories they conjured were weaker, like the fading of a musical note. They didn't possess the power they'd once had. I knew I no longer needed them. With five presses of my thumb they were gone. The anchor rope that was the past, finally cut.

This wasn't the reason I'd come up here, though. I needed to find something.

I started on one corner of the rock and walked slowly across it, looking as I went. I carried on searching, but after twenty minutes I'd found nothing. Maybe I needed glasses too.

I was about to give up when I saw it.

'Dex, come here,' I cried.

Dexter ran over to see what all the fuss was about. There, freshly carved into the side of Cow Rock:

Spider + Tyler. Canny swimmers.

People had been coming up here for years and years, and they wanted the world to know it. There were scores of names carved into the rocks, some from the early 1800s. The Cow Rock was one giant class register. This message would baffle people for hundreds of years to come.

Spider must have brought a hammer and chisel, by the looks of it, determined that the summer we'd spent together would never be forgotten. The girl who no one wanted had found someone. That someone was me, and Spider had made sure she and I would be here for ever.

I stood staring at the carving, smiling.

'I'm so glad I met you.'

A soft wind blew up from the valley, as the sun, caressing a distant hilltop, prepared to slip away.

'Come on, Dex, time to go.'

And we headed down the steep path towards home.

Centrepoint
is the UK's leading youth
homelessness charity.

*

If you're sofa surfing, homeless or at risk
you can contact the Centrepoint Helpline
for free on 0808 800 0661. Support is
also available online via a chat service
at https://centrepoint.org.uk/helpline.

Acknowledgements

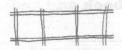

For their wise words, patience and unwavering support I'd like to thank: my agent, Davinia Andrew-Lynch, my editor and publisher, Fiona Kennedy, editor Lauren Atherton, and everyone at Head of Zeus.

For helping me see into the world of the homeless a big thanks to: Camilla Wheal and everyone at Kingston Churches Action on Homeless; Janna Watt, George Olney, and Elisabeth Seifert at Crisis; Grace Hetherington at Centre Point; Eric Richardson and the team at Simon on the Streets, Leeds.

Not forgetting, the many homeless people I met. Their stoicism and courage inspired me more than they'll ever know.

**Available in paperback,
ebook and audio**

Winner of the YA Sheffield Children's Book Award 2019
Winner of the Redbridge Children's Book Award 2019
Shortlisted for the Waterstones Children's Book Prize 2019
Shortlisted for the Bristol Teen Book Award 2019
Longlisted for the Branford Boase 2019
Nominated for the CILIP Carnegie Prize 2019
World Book Night Title 2019

'Touching and compelling to the end… It has sweetness and comedy, despite the gravity of its theme.'
Sunday Times, **Book of the Week**

'It's hard to think of a work I've read for young people in recent times that has so much heart and humour, yet manages to explore such darkness… I heartily recommend this for all teens.'
The Herald, **Books of the Year**

'An assured debut… Danny's honest distinctive voice brings humour and hope.'
The Bookseller

'For pitch-perfect teenage voices, you can't go wrong with Malcolm Duffy's *Me Mam. Me Dad. Me.*'
Irish Times, **Books of the Year**

'The subject might be harrowing, but Duffy handles it with a light touch.'
Northern Echo

'Never once does the authenticity of the narration waver… The immediacy of the text is potent.'
Books For Keeps

'A powerful story of filial love when domestic violence gets in the way. An unforgettable central character and a truthful ending make for a truly impactful read.'
The Bookbag

'Stories like Danny's are important. Duffy explores the themes of domestic violence, isolation, and growing up with sensitivity, energy and heart.'
Armadillo

'All the stars to _Me Mam. Me Dad. Me._ A tragic, funny, heart-breaking, hopeful look at domestic violence. Such a great character voice and fabulous NE setting.'
Eileen Armstrong, School Librarian

'Very immediate, well-told, well-paced... I really loved Danny. I loved his Geordie voice.'
Down the Rabbit Hole

'A real poignant and heart-wrenching story of not just Danny, but many kids who witness domestic abuse and their struggle to cope with their reality.'
The Mrs Literary Blog

'Reading a book in the dialect that surrounds me day to day was such a pleasure. _Me Mam. Me Dad. Me._ is heart-breaking and tackles some difficult topics, but it manages to stay accessible and engaging.'
Tea Party Princess Blog

'It is a story that, in the end, is happy and restorative, but on the way has travelled many journeys and faced many challenges. I didn't just like it, I loved it.'
Mike Riddall, Zephyr Review Crew

Now enjoy reading the first two chapters of

One

•

It was the day the clocks went back. That's when I decided to kill him.

I'd been playing football with me mates, Barry Mossman, Ben Simpson and Carl Hedgley from school. Gavin Latham should have been there too but his mam took him for a haircut. We were in the park near the cemetery. Just did corners and penalties. You can't have a proper game with four.

It got too dark to see the ball. Told Barry he should have brought his white one. So we went home. I normally go on me bike, but it had a flatty. Bounced me ball all the way. Three hundred and eighty-seven bounces it was. Counted them. Nearly gave up a few times, but it gave me something to do.

Went round the side of the house, through the gate and in the back door. Mam always leaves it open when I'm out. The second I opened the door I heard it – crying, big crying like you hear on the telly sometimes. Thought at first maybe it was the telly. Put the ball next to the pedal bin, went to the front room, and peeped in. The telly was off. Black. Nobody there.

Stood still for a bit and listened. The crying was coming from upstairs. Sounded a bit like me mam, but was weird, quiet one minute and dead loud the next, like someone was messing with the volume. Went slow to the top of the stairs. Crept to her door on tippy-toes and listened. That's where it was coming from. Was her all right, definitely her. The noise made me guts feel funny, like I was on a roller coaster. Had a feeling I knew what had happened. Hoped I was wrong. I needed to find out. Took a breath and turned the handle.

Locked.

Who puts a lock on a bedroom door?

Knocked.

'Mam.'

The crying was too big.

'Mam, it's Danny. What's the marra?' I shouted.

The crying stopped, dead quick.

'Go downstairs, Danny,' she screamed. The way her voice sounded scared me more than the crying.

'Y'alreet, Mam?'

Stupid question.

'Yes.'

Stupid answer.

'Course she wasn't all right. You don't cry like that when you're all right. Not unless there's something really sad on telly. Or somebody's dead. Or a pet.

'Have you hurt yourself?'

'Go away, Danny, please.'

Wanted to.

Didn't.

'What's happened?'

'Nothing.'

But I knew it was something. Not even a cissy cries like that, and me mam's not one of those. I saw her shout at a bloke in the supermarket once. Was next to the crisps. He had tattoos all over his bald head. He'd bashed her trolley but never said sorry, just eyeballed her. She shouted at him and crossed her arms. Wouldn't back down. I was dead proud of her.

'Do you want a cup of tea, Mam?'

Never heard her say no to a cup of tea.

'No.'

Weird.

'Where's Callum?'

I heard a laugh. But it was the type you do when something's not funny.

'Where do you think?' she said.

Knew the answer to that one.

'Shall I call Aunty Tina?'

'No.'

'Uncle Greg?'

'No'

'What about Uncle Martin?'

'No,' shouted me mam, even louder. 'I want you to go away.'

And then the crying started again.

I just wanted to know what had happened, that's all, but she's me mam so I did as I was told. Went downstairs and turned on the telly. Hoped there might be football on, but couldn't find any anywhere. Must have been my unlucky day, there's always football on somewhere. Found another channel, with lions. I like lions, me. They were scrapping. I turned the sound up. The fighting drowned out me mam.

It was tea time. But there was no tea. This was the first time this had happened. Ever. Mam always makes me tea, even when she's got the flu or had too much red wine. But for once I was glad she'd not made any. I wasn't hungry. You can't eat when your guts are clenched as tight as a fist. Not when you don't know what's happened to your mam.

I got bored with the lions pawing each other and called Amy. Just hearing her voice would make me feel better. But her phone was off. I left a message saying I hoped she was okay.

Looked out of the window. It was dark outside now, really dark. That's what happens when you change the clocks. Stupid idea if you ask me. Why would you want it to be dark at tea time one day when the day before it wasn't? Doesn't make a scrap of sense. I watched some more telly. This time I turned the sound off so I could listen for me mam. Rugby was on. Don't like rugby. It's even more stupid with the sound off.

Just when I thought nothing would ever happen, it did. I heard soft footsteps on the stairs, like a burglar would make. It was me mam, coming to make me tea.

'Mam?'

'Stay in there, son,' she said. 'Just stay in there, please.'

I heard her slippers shuffling to the kitchen, like she was dragging something heavy. Then she blew her nose.

She'd told me to stay put, but I couldn't. Had to know. Opened the door dead quiet and went in slow motion down the hall. The kitchen door was shut. I was scared, like watching a horror film, when you don't know what's in the room. I turned the handle, pushed the door a bit, and peeped in.

Me mam was just standing there, her back to me, looking out into the dark. But she didn't have to turn. I saw her face mirrored in the window, covered in great big bruises, one of her eyes as black as the sky outside.

She reached across, grabbed a kitchen towel, and spat into it. The white paper turned red.

Mam slumped over the sink, her arms across her stomach like she had a cramp, and started crying again.

That's when I knew I had to kill him.

Two

• •

I love me mam, me.

Just as well. For years we'd been living together in the same flat. No relatives. No boyfriend. No bairns. No lodgers. Just us.

I reckon she'd do anything for me. Always got something lush to microwave for me tea. Always lets me go on her laptop. Always makes sure me football kit's clean. Socks the right way round. Always buys me the top thing off me birthday list, even though I know she's not minted. And always gives me a goodnight hug, even when I've done nowt to deserve it. Bet there's not many mams do all that.

I think I drive her mad sometimes, but she usually just folds her arms and blows out hot air. She hardly ever goes mental. I get shouted at enough at school, so it's good to live in a shout-free zone.

I bet she secretly wishes she had a daughter. But if she does she never lets on. Just has to listen to me football talk with her wish-he'd-talk-about-something-else-face. The same face I've got when she talks about clothes.

But me mam's not just kind, she's also dead pretty. Short, but pretty. I reckon she could be a model if it wasn't for the chocolate biscuits. But can't see her ever ditching them. They're her number one drug.

'Danny, take them away from me,' she says.

If she doesn't want them, why does she get them out in the first place?

So instead of being a model, she works in a call centre. She's got a canny voice, me mam. Think that's how she got her job.

When I was little me mam and me used to live with me gran and granda down the road in Dunston. I liked living there. It was a house with people always coming and going. Neighbours, friends, relatives, they'd all pop in for any reason whatsoever and the house would be full of noise. Me gran's one of those people who never runs out of things to say. If talking was in the Olympics she'd win a gold.

But when I was about nine we had to leave.

'We're gonna have to move, Danny. We've outgrown this place.'

Me mam and me used to share the same room. Said now that I was bigger it was time we got our own place. So she went and got a flat off the council in Low Fell.

The council have got millions of flats and houses. I don't know why they had to go and give us that one. It wasn't like me gran's house. No garden. No upstairs. It just had four rooms. Five, if you count the toilet. It got that cold in the winter me mam and me would get dressed for going out, even when we were stopping in. And the walls got wet for no good reason. But it had two good things about it. I had me own bedroom, and it was near me school, so I could stop in bed till the very last second.

We didn't get many people coming to our flat. Maybe me mam didn't have enough chairs. Or maybe she was embarrassed about the temperature or the wet. I missed all the people who used to come to me gran's. And I don't see so much of her and granda now. Shame. Love me gran almost as much as me mam. She's dead huggy. Love me granda too. But he doesn't give any hugs. He's got dementia.

But I still got to see everyone. Whenever it was a birthday or something we'd all get together for a party at me mam's sister's house. Aunty Tina's different from me mam. She's got a car, a swanky house and a posh voice. Aunty Tina doesn't live round here. She lives over the Tyne in a place that's that big they need a cleaner.

Uncle Greg must have the best job ever. Or he's a criminal. They've got two bairns, Tabitha and Marcus. Also posh.

Then there's the relatives we don't see much, like me mam's cousins who live in Manchester, and her brother, Uncle Martin, who lost his job and went to live in Darlington with Aunty Sheila. They haven't got any bairns. Maybe that's why they're so happy when they see me. Like people who haven't got a dog, when they see a dog.

Aye, me life with me mam wasn't the sort you'd make a film about, but it was canny. I had me mates. I had me football. I had me relatives. I had me mam. She loved me. I loved her. Was happy for that to go on and on and on and on.

And then me world went upside down.

National Domestic Abuse Helpline

If you or someone you know has been affected
by the issues raised in this story, you can contact
the Freephone 24 Hour National Domestic
Violence Helpline, run in partnership between
Women's Aid and Refuge, on

0808 2000 247